"I thought you were coming in," Parker said.

"Well, I have to change first."

"Do you?" he asked with a devilish grin.

"Oh, Parker, no—" Shawna said, just as two strong hands gripped her ankles and pulled her into the water, wool skirt, silk blouse, and all.

"You're despicable!" she sputtered, surfacing, her hair drenched.

"Probably."

"And cruel . . . and heartless . . . and . . ."

"Adorable," he suggested with a laugh.

"That, too," she admitted, lost in his eyes as he gazed at her. Heart pounding erratically, she could barely breathe as his head lowered and his lips brushed erotically over hers.

"So are you." His arm gripped her fiercely, possessively. "Lord, so are you."

Knowing she was playing with fire, Shawna was too caught up in the wonder of being held by Parker, the feel of his wet body against hers. She'd waited so long for just this moment— to have him want her again. . . .

WHAT ARE *LOVESWEPT* ROMANCES?

They are stories of true romance and touching emotion. We believe those two very important ingredients are constants in our highly sensual and very believable stories in the *LOVESWEPT* line. Our goal is to give you, the reader, stories of consistently high quality that may sometimes make you laugh, sometimes make you cry, but are always fresh and creative and contain many delightful surprises within their pages.

Most romance fans read an enormous number of books. Those they truly love, they keep. Others may be traded with friends and soon forgotten. We hope that each *LOVESWEPT* romance will be a treasure—a "keeper." We will always try to publish

LOVE STORIES YOU'LL NEVER FORGET
BY AUTHORS YOU'LL ALWAYS REMEMBER

The Editors

LOVESWEPT® • 264

Susan Crose
The Brass Ring

 BANTAM BOOKS
TORONTO • NEW YORK • LONDON • SYDNEY • AUCKLAND

THE BRASS RING
A Bantam Book / July 1988

If you would be interested in receiving protective vinyl
covers for your Loveswept books, please write to this address
for information:

Loveswept
Bantam Books
P.O. Box 985
Hicksville, NY 11802

ISBN 0-553-21907-3

Published simultaneously in the United States and Canada

Bantam Books are published by Bantam Books, a division
of Bantam Doubleday Dell Publishing Group, Inc. Its trademark, consisting of the words "Bantam Books" and the
portrayal of a rooster, is Registered in U.S. Patent and
Trademark Office and in other countries. Marca Registrada.
Bantam Books, 666 Fifth Avenue, New York, New York 10103.

One

The old merry-go-round picked up speed, ancient gears grinding as black smoke spewed from the diesel engine and clouded the summer-blue Oregon sky.

Shawna McGuire clung to the neck of her wooden mount and glanced over her shoulder. Her heart swelled at the sight of Parker Harrison. Tall, with the broad shoulders of a natural athlete and brown hair streaked gold by the sun, he sat astride a glossy striped tiger. His blue eyes were gazing possessively at her and a camera swung from his neck.

Shawna grinned shamelessly. Tomorrow morning she and Parker would be married!

The carousel spun faster. Colors of pink, blue, and yellow blurred together.

"Reach, Shawna! Come on, you can do it!" Parker yelled, his deep voice difficult to hear above the piped music of the calliope and the sputtering engine.

Grinning, her honey-gold hair billowing away from her face, she saw him wink at her, then focus his camera and aim.

"Go for it, *Doctor*!" he called.

The challenge was on and Shawna glanced forward again, her green eyes fixed on the brass ring with fluttering pastel ribbons, the prize that hung precariously near the speeding carousel. She stretched her fingers, grabbed as she passed the ring and swiped into the air, coming up with nothing and nearly falling off her painted white stallion in the bargain. She heard Parker's laughter and looked back just in time to see him snatch the prize. A big, gloating smile spread easily across his square jaw and the look he sent her made her heart pound wildly.

She thought about her plans for the wedding the following morning. It was almost too good to be true. In less than twenty-four hours, under the rose arbor at Pioneer Church, she'd become Mrs. Parker Harrison and they would be bound for a week-long honeymoon in the Caribbean! No busy hospital schedules, no double shifts, no phones or patients—just Parker.

She glimpsed Parker stuffing the ring and ribbons into the front pocket of his jeans as the merry-go-round slowed.

"That's how it's done," he said, cupping his hands over his mouth so that she could hear him.

"Insufferable, arrogant—" she muttered, but a dimple creased her cheek and she laughed gaily, clasping her fingers around the post supporting her mount and tossing back her head. Her long hair brushed against her shoulders and she could hear the warm sound of Parker's laughter. She was young and in love—nothing could be more perfect.

When the ride ended she climbed off her glazed white horse and felt Parker's strong arms surround her. "That was a feeble attempt if I ever saw one," he whispered into her ear as he lifted her to the ground.

"We all can't be professional athletes," she teased, looking up at him through gold-tipped lashes. "Some of us have to set goals, you know, to achieve higher intellectual and humanistic rewards."

"Bull!"

"Bull?" she repeated, arching a golden brow.

"Save that for someone who'll believe it, Doctor. I won and you're burned."

"Well, maybe just a little," she admitted, her eyes shining. "But it is comforting to know that should I ever quit my practice, and if you gave up completely on tennis, we could depend on your income as a professional ring-grabber."

"I'll get you for that one, Dr. McGuire," he promised, squeezing her small waist, his hand catching in the cotton folds of her sundress. "And my vengeance will be swift and powerful and drop you to your knees!"

"Promises, promises!" she quipped, dashing away from him and winding quickly through the crowd. Dry grass brushed against her ankles and several times her sandals caught on an exposed pebble, but she finally reached a refreshment booth with Parker right on her heels. "A bag of buttered popcorn and a sack of peanuts," she said to the vendor standing under the striped awnings. She felt out of breath and flushed, and her eyes glimmered mischievously. "And this guy," she motioned to Parker as he approached, "will foot the bill."

"Henpecked already," Parker muttered, delving into his wallet and handing a five-dollar bill to the vendor. Someday—" he said, blue eyes dancing as he shucked open a peanut and tossed the nut into his mouth.

"Someday what?" she challenged, her pulse leaping when his eyes fixed on her lips. For a minute she thought he was going to kiss her right there in the middle of the crowd. If he did, she wouldn't stop him. She couldn't. She loved him too much.

"Just you wait, lady—" he warned, his voice low and throaty, the vein in the side of his neck pulsing.

Shawna's heart began to thud crazily.

"For what?"

A couple of giggling teenage girls approached, breaking the magical spell. "Mr. Harrison?" the taller, red-haired girl asked, while her friend in braces blushed.

Parker looked over his shoulder and twisted around. "Yes?"

"I told you it was him!" the girl in braces said, nearly jumping up and down in her excitement. Her brown eyes gleamed in anticipation.

"Could we, uh, would you mind—" the redhead fumbled in her purse "—could we get your autograph?"

"Sure," Parker said, taking the scraps of paper and pen that had been shoved into his hand and scribbling out his name.

"I'm Sara and this is Kelly. Uh—Sara without an 'h.' "

"Got it!" Parker finished writing.

"Is, um, Brad here?"

" 'Fraid not," Parker admitted, the corner of his mouth lifting as he snapped the cap back onto the pen.

"Too bad," Sara murmured, obviously disappointed as she tucked her pen and paper into her purse.

But Kelly smiled widely, displaying the wires covering her teeth. "Gee, thanks!"

The two girls waved and took off, giggling to themselves.

"The price of fame," Parker said teasingly.

"Not too bad for a has-been," Shawna commented dryly, unable to hide the pride in her voice. "But it didn't hurt that you're Brad Lomax's coach. He's the star now, you know."

Parker grinned crookedly. "Admit it, McGuire, you're still sore 'cause you didn't get the ring." Draping his arm possessively around her shoulders, he hugged her close.

"Maybe just a little," she said with a happy sigh. The day had been perfect despite the humidity. High overhead, the boughs of tall firs swayed in the sultry summer breeze and dark clouds drifted in from the west.

Shawna's feet barely hit the ground as they walked through the "Fair from Yesteryear." Sprawled over several acres of farmland in the foothills of the Cascade Mountains, the dun-colored tents, flashy rides, and booths were backdropped by spectacular mountains. Muted calliope music filled the summer air, and barkers, hawking their wares and games, shouted over the noise of the crowd. The smells of horses, sawdust, popcorn, and caramel wafted through the crowded, tent-lined fields that served as fair grounds.

"Want to test your strength?" Shawna asked, glancing up at Parker and pointing to a lumberjack who was hoisting a heavy mallet over his head. Swinging the hammer with all of his might, the brawny man grunted loudly. The mallet crashed against a springboard and hurled a hearty weight halfway up a tall pole.

Parker's lips curved cynically. "I'll pass. Don't want to ruin my tennis arm, you know."

"Sure."

Parker ran his fingers through his sun-streaked hair. "There is another reason," he admitted.

She arched an eyebrow quizzically. "Which is?"

"I think I'll save my strength for tomorrow night." His voice lowered and his eyes darkened mysteriously. "There's this certain lady who's expecting all of my attention and physical prowess."

"Is that right?" She popped a piece of popcorn into his mouth and grinned. "Then you'd better not disappoint her."

"I won't," he promised, his gaze shifting to her mouth.

Shawna swallowed with difficulty. Whenever he looked at her that way, so sensual and determined, her heart always started beating a rapid double-time. She had to glance away, over his shoulder to a short, plump woman who was standing in front of a tent.

Catching Shawna's eye, the woman called, "How about I read your fortune?" With bright scarves wrapped around her head, painted fingernails, and dangling hooped earrings, she waved Shawna and Parker inside.

"I don't know—"

"Why not?" Parker argued, propelling her into the darkened tent. Smelling of sawdust and cloying perfume, the tent was dark and close. Shawna sat on a dusty pillow near a small table and wondered what had possessed her to enter. The floor was covered with sawdust and straw, the only illumination coming from a slit in the top of the canvas. The place gave her the creeps.

Placing a five-dollar bill on the corner of the table, Parker sat next to Shawna, one arm still draped casually over her shoulders, his long legs crossed Indian style.

The money quickly disappeared into the voluminous folds of the Gypsy woman's skirt as she settled onto a mound of pillows on the other side of the table. "You first?" she asked, flashing Shawna a friendly, gold-capped smile.

Shrugging, Shawna glanced at Parker before meeting the Gypsy woman's gaze. "Sure. Why not?"

"Good!" Lady Fate clapped her wrinkled palms together. "Now, let me read your palm." Taking Shawna's hand in hers, she gently stroked the smooth skin, tracing the lines of Shawna's palm with her long fingers.

"I see you have worked long and hard in your job."

That much was true, Shawna thought wryly. She'd spent more hours than she wanted to count as a bartender while going to college and medical school. It had been years of grueling work, late shifts, and early morning classes, but finally, just this past year, she'd become a full-fledged internist. Even now, juggling time between her clinic and the hospital, she was working harder than she'd ever expected.

"And you have a happy family."

"Yes," Shawna admitted proudly. "A brother and my parents."

The woman nodded, as if she saw their faces in Shawna's palm. "You will live a long and fruitful life," she said thickly and then her fingers moved and she traced another line on Shawna's hand, only to stop short. Her face clouded, her old lips pursed and she dropped Shawna's wrist as quickly as she had taken it earlier. "Your time is over," she said gently, kindness sparking in her old brown eyes.

"What?"

"Next," Lady Fate said, calling toward the flap used as a door.

"That's all?" Shawna repeated, surprised. She didn't know much about fortune-telling, but she'd just begun to enjoy the game and some of her five-dollar future was missing.

"Yes. I've told you everything. Now, if you'll excuse me—"

"Wait a minute. What about my love life?" Glancing at Parker in the shadowed room, Shawna winked.

Lady Fate hesitated.

"I thought you could see everything," Shawna said. "That's what your sign says."

"There are some things better left unknown," the woman whispered softly as she started to stand.

"I can handle it," Shawna said, but felt a little uneasy.

"Really, you don't want to know," Lady Fortune declared, pursing her red lips and starting to stand.

"Of course I do," Shawna insisted. Though she didn't really believe in any of this mumbo jumbo, she wanted to get her money's worth. "I want to know everything." Shawna thrust her open palm back to the woman.

"She's very stubborn," Parker interjected.

"So I see." The fortune teller slowly sat down on her pillows as she closed Shawna's fingers, staring straight into her eyes. "I see there is a very important man in your life—you love him dearly, too much, perhaps."

"And?" Shawna asked, disgusted with herself when

she felt the hairs on the back of her neck prickle with dread.

"And you will lose him," the woman said sadly, glancing at Parker and then standing to brush some of the straw from her skirt. "Now go."

"Come on," Parker said, his eyes glinting mischievously. "It's time you got rid of that love of your life and started concentrating on me." He took Shawna by the hand and pulled her from the dark tent.

Outside, the air was hot and muggy but a refreshing change from the sticky interior of the tiny canvas booth. "You set her up to that, didn't you?" Shawna accused, still uneasy as she glanced back at the fortune-teller's tent.

"No way! Don't tell me you believed all of that baloney she tried to peddle you!"

"Of course not, but it was kind of creepy." Shuddering, she rubbed her bare arms despite the heat.

"And way off base." Laughing, he tugged on her hand and led her through a thicket of fir trees, away from the crowd and the circus atmosphere of the fair.

The heavy boughs offered a little shade and privacy and cooled the sweat beading on the back of Shawna's neck.

"You didn't believe her, did you?" he asked, his eyes delving deep into hers.

"No, but—"

"Just wait 'til the medical board gets wind of this!"

She couldn't help but smile as she twisted her hair into a loose rope and held it over her head, and off her neck. "You're laughing at me."

"Maybe a little." Stepping closer, he pinned her back against the rough bark of a Douglas fir, his arms resting lightly on her shoulders. "You deserve it, too, after all that guff you gave me about that damned brass ring."

"Guilty as charged," she admitted. She let her hair fall free and wrapped her hands around his lean, hard waist. Even beneath his light shirt, she could feel the ripple of his muscles as he shifted.

"Good." Taking the brass ring from his pocket, he slipped the oversized band onto her wrist. "With this ring, I thee wed," he said quietly, watching the ribbons flutter over her arm.

Shawna had to blink back some stupid tears of happiness that wet her lashes. "I can't wait," she murmured, "for the real thing."

"Neither can I." Placing his forehead against hers, he stared at the dimpled smile playing on her lips.

Shawna's pulse leaped. His warm breath fanned her face, his fingers twined lazily in a long strand of her honey-gold hair and his mouth curved upward in a sardonic smile. "And now, Dr. McGuire, prepare yourself. I intend to have my way with you!" he said menacingly.

"Right here?" she asked innocently.

"For starters." He brushed his lips slowly over hers and Shawna sighed into his mouth.

She felt warm all over and weak in the knees. He kissed her eyelids and throat and she moaned, parting her lips expectantly. His hands felt strong and powerful and she knew that Parker would always take care of her and protect her. Deep inside, fires of desire that only he could spark ignited.

"I love you," she whispered, the wind carrying her words away as it lifted her hair away from her face.

"And I love you." Raising his head, he stared into

her passion-glazed eyes. "And tomorrow night, I'm going to show you just how much."

"Do we really have to wait?" she whispered, disappointment pouting her lips.

"Not much longer—but we had a deal, remember?"

"It was stupid."

"Probably," he agreed. "And it's been hell." His angular features grew taut. "But weren't you the one who said, 'Everything meaningful is worth the wait'?"

"That's a butchered version of it, but yes," she said.

"And we've made it this far."

"It's been agony," she admitted. "The next time I have such lofty, idealistic and stupid ideas, go ahead and shoot me."

Grinning, he placed a kiss on her forehead. "I suppose this means that I'll have to give up my mistress."

"Your *what*!" she sputtered, knowing that he was teasing. *His mistress!* This mystery woman—a pure fantasy—had always been a joke between them, a joke that hurt more than it should have. "Oooh, you're absolutely the most arrogant, self-centered, egotistical—"

Capturing her wrists, he held them high over her head with one hand. "Go on," he urged, eyes slowly inching down her body, past her flashing green eyes and pursed lips, to the hollow of her throat where her pulse was fluttering rapidly, then lower still, to the soft mounds of her breasts, pushed proudly forward against apricot-colored cotton, rising and falling with each of her shallow breaths.

"—self-important, presumptuous, insolent bastard I've ever met!"

Lowering his head, he kissed the sensitive circle of bones at the base of her throat and she felt liquid inside. "Leave anything out?" he asked, his breath warm against her already overheated skin.

"A million things!"

"Such as?"

"Mistress," she repeated and then sucked in a sharp breath when she felt his moist tongue touch her throat. "Stop it," she said weakly, wanting to protest but unable.

"Aren't you the woman who was just begging for more a few minutes ago?"

"Parker—"

Then he cut off her protest with his mouth slanting swiftly over hers, his body pressed urgently against her. He kissed her with the passion that she'd seen burning in him ever since the first time they'd met. Her back was pinned to the trunk of the tree, her hands twined anxiously around his neck, wanton desire flowing from his lips to hers.

His hips were thrust against hers and she could feel the intensity of his passion, his heat radiating against her. "Please—" she whispered and he groaned.

His tongue rimmed her lips and then tasted of the sweetness within her open mouth.

"Parker—" She closed her eyes and moaned softly.

Suddenly every muscle in his body tensed and he released her as quickly as he'd captured her. Swearing, he stepped away from her. "You're dangerous, you know that, don't you?" His hands were shaking when he pushed the hair from his eyes. "I—I think we'd better go," he said thickly, clearly trying to quell the desire pounding in his brain.

Swallowing hard, she nodded. She could feel a hot

flush staining her cheeks, knew her heart was racing out of control, and had trouble catching her breath. "But tomorrow, Mr. Harrison—you're not going to get away so easily."

"Don't tease me," he warned, his mouth a thin line of self-control.

"Never," she promised, forest-green eyes serious.

Linking his fingers with hers, he pulled her toward the parking lot. "I think we'd better get out of here. If I remember correctly, we have a wedding rehearsal and a dinner to get through tonight."

"That's right," she groaned, combing her tangled hair with her fingers, as they threaded their way through the cars parked in uneven rows. "You know, I should have listened to you when you wanted to elope."

"Next time, you'll know."

"There won't be a next time," she vowed as he opened the door of his Jeep and she slid into the sweltering interior. "You're going to be stuck with me for life!"

"I wouldn't have it any other way." Once behind the wheel, he cranked open the windows and turned on the ignition.

"Even if you have to give up your mistress?"

Coughing, he glanced at her. One corner of his mouth lifted cynically as he maneuvered the car out of the bumpy, cracked field that served as a parking lot. "The things I do for love," he muttered and then switched on the radio and shifted gears.

Shawna stared out the window at the passing countryside. In the distance, dark clouds had begun to gather around the rugged slopes of Mount Hood. Shadows lengthened across the hilly, dry farmland.

Dry, golden pastures turned dark as the wind picked up. Grazing cattle lifted their heads at the scent of the approaching storm and weeds and wild flowers along the fencerows bent double in the muggy breeze.

"Looks like a storm brewing." Parker glanced at the hard, dry ground and frowned. "I guess we could use a little rain."

"But not tonight or tomorrow," Shawna said. "Not on our wedding day." *Tomorrow*, she thought with a smile. She tried to ignore the Gypsy woman's grim prediction and the promise of rain. "Tomorrow will be perfect!"

". . . and may you have all the happiness you deserve. To the bride and groom!" Jake said, casting a smile at his sister and holding his wineglass high in the air.

Hoisting her glass, Shawna beamed, watching her dark-haired brother through adoring eyes.

"Here, here," the rest of the guests chimed in, glasses clinking, laughter and cheery conversation filling the large banquet room of the Edwardian Hotel in downtown Portland. The room was crowded with family and friends, all members of the wedding party. After a rehearsal marred by only a few hitches, and a lovely veal dinner, the wine, toasts and fellowship were flowing freely in the elegant room.

"How was that?" Jake asked, taking his chair.

"Eloquent," Shawna admitted, smiling at her brother. "I didn't know you had it in you."

"That's because you never listened to me," he quipped, and then, setting his elbows on the table, winked at Parker. "I hope you have better luck keeping her in line."

"I will," Parker predicted, loosening his tie.

"Hey, wait a minute," Shawna protested, but laughed and sipped from a glass of cold Chablis.

"I can't wait until tomorrow," Gerri, Shawna's best friend, said with a smile. "I never thought I'd see this day, when someone actually convinced the good doctor to walk down the aisle." Shaking her auburn hair, Gerri leaned back and lit a cigarette, clicking her lighter shut to add emphasis to her words.

"I'm not married to my work," Shawna protested.

"Not anymore. But you were. Back in those days when you were in med school, you were no fun. I repeat: *No fun!*"

Parker hugged his bride-to-be. "I intend to change all that, starting tomorrow!"

"Oh, you do, do you?" Shawna said, her gaze narrowing on him. "I'll have you know, Mr. Harrison, that *you'll* be the one toeing the line."

"This should be good," Jake decided. "Parker Harrison under a woman's thumb."

"I'll drink to that!" Brad Lomax, Parker's most famous student, leaned over Shawna's shoulder, spilling some of his drink on the linen tablecloth. His black hair was mussed, his tie already lost, and the smell of bourbon was heavy on his breath. He'd been in a bad mood all evening and had chosen to drown whatever problems he had in a bottle.

"Maybe you should slow down a little," Parker suggested, as the boy swayed over the table.

"What? In the middle of this celebration? No way, man!" To add emphasis to his words, he downed his drink and signaled to the waiter for another.

Parker's eyes grew serious. "Really, Brad, you've had enough."

"Never enough!" He grabbed a glass of champagne from a passing waiter. "Put it on his tab!" Brad said, cocking his thumb at Parker. "This is his las' night of freedom! Helluva waste if ya ask me!"

Jake glanced from Parker to Brad and back again. "Maybe I should take him home," he suggested.

But Brad reached into his pocket, fumbled around and finally withdrew his keys. "I can do it myself," he said testily.

"Brad—"

"I'll go when I'm damned good and ready." Leaning forward, he placed one arm around Parker, the other around Shawna. "You know, I jus' might end up married myself," he decided, grinning sloppily.

"I'd like to be there on the day some girl gets her hooks into you," Parker said. "It'll never happen."

Brad laughed, splashing his drink again. "Guess again," he said, slumping against Shawna.

"Why don't you tell me about it on the way home?" Parker suggested. He helped Brad back to his feet.

"But the party's not over—"

"It is for us. We've got a pretty full schedule tomorrow. I don't want you so hung over that you miss the ceremony."

"I won't be!"

"Right. 'Cause I'm taking you home right now." He set Brad's drink on the table and took the keys from his hand. Then, leaning close to Shawna, he kissed her forehead. "I'll see you in the morning, okay?"

"Eleven o'clock, sharp," she replied, looking up at him, her eyes shining.

"Wouldn't miss it for the world."

"Me neither," Brad agreed, his arm still slung over

Parker's broad shoulders as they headed for the door. " 'Sides, I need to talk to you, need some advice," he added confidentially to Parker.

"So what else is new?"

"Be careful," Jake suggested. "It's raining cats and dogs out there—the first time in a couple months. The roads are bound to be slick."

"Will do," Parker agreed.

Jake watched them leave, his eyes narrowing on Parker's broad shoulders. "I don't see why Parker puts up with Brad," he said, frowning into his drink.

Shawna lifted a shoulder. "You know Brad is Parker's star student, supposedly seeded ninth in the country. Parker expects him to follow in his footsteps, make it to the top—win the grand slam. The whole nine yards, so to speak."

"That's football, Sis. Not tennis."

"You know what I mean."

"He's that good?" Obviously, Jake didn't believe it, and Shawna understood why. As a psychiatrist, he'd seen more than his share of kids who'd gotten too much too fast and couldn't handle the fame or money.

Leaning back in her chair, Shawna quoted, "The best natural athlete that Parker's ever seen."

Jake shook his head, glancing again at the door through which Parker and Brad had disappeared. "Maybe so, but the kid's got a temper and a chip on his shoulder the size of the Rock of Gibraltar."

"Thank you for your professional opinion, Dr. McGuire."

"Is that a nice way of saying 'butt out'?" Jake asked.

Shawna shook her head. "No, it's a nice way of saying, let's keep the conversation light—no heavy stuff, okay? I'm getting married tomorrow."

"How could I forget?" Clicking the rim of his glass to hers, he whispered, "And I wish you all the luck in the world." He took a sip of his wine. "You know what the best part of this marriage is, don't you?"

"Living with Parker?"

"Nope. The fact that this is the last day there will be two Dr. McGuires working at Columbia Memorial. No more mixed-up messages or calls."

"That's right. From now on, I'll be Dr. Harrison." She wrinkled her nose a bit. "Doesn't have the same ring to it, does it?"

"Sounds great to me."

"Me, too," she admitted, looking into her wine glass and smiling at the clear liquid within. "Me, too."

She felt a light tap on her shoulder and looked up. Her father was standing behind her chair. A tall, rotund man, he was dressed in his best suit, and a sad smile curved his lips. "How about a dance with my favorite girl?" he asked.

"You've got it," she said, pushing back her chair and taking his hand. "But after that, I'm going home."

"Tired?"

"Uh-huh, and I want to look my best tomorrow."

"Don't worry. You'll be the prettiest bride ever to walk down that aisle."

"The wedding's going to be in the rose garden, remember?" She laughed, and her father's face pulled together.

"I don't suppose I can talk you into saying your vows in front of the altar?"

"Nope. Outside," she said, glancing out the window into the dark night. Rain shimmered on the window panes. "I don't care if this blasted rain keeps falling, we're going to be married under the arbor in the rose garden of the church."

"You always were stubborn," he muttered, twirling her around the floor. "Just like your mother."

"Some people say I'm a chip off the old block, and they aren't talking about Mom."

Malcolm McGuire laughed as he waltzed his daughter around the room. "I know this is the eleventh hour, but sometimes I wonder if you're rushing things a bit. You haven't known Parker all that long."

"Too late, Dad. If you wanted to talk me out of this, you shouldn't have waited this long," she pointed out.

"Don't get me wrong; I like Parker."

"Good, because you're stuck with him as a son-in-law."

"I just hope you're not taking on too much," he said thoughtfully. "You're barely out of med school and you have a new practice. Now you're taking on the responsibilities of becoming a wife—"

"And a mother?" she teased.

Malcolm's eyebrows quirked. "I know you want children, but that can come later."

"I'm already twenty-eight!"

"That's not ancient, Shawna. You and Parker, you're both young."

"And in love. So quit worrying," she admonished with a fond grin. "I'm a big girl now. I can take care of myself. And if I can't, Parker will."

"He'd better," her father said, winking broadly. "Or he'll have to answer to me!"

When the strains of the waltz drifted away, he patted Shawna's arm and escorted her back to her chair. He glanced around the room as she slipped her arms through the sleeves of her coat. "So where is that husband-to-be of yours? Don't tell me he already skipped out."

"Very funny." She lifted her hair out of the collar of her raincoat and said, "He took Brad Lomax home a little earlier. But don't worry, Dad, he'll be there tomorrow. I'll see you then."

Tucking her purse under her arm, she hurried down the stairs, unwilling to wait for the elevator. On the first floor, she dashed through the lobby of the old Victorian hotel, and shouldered open the heavy wood door.

The rain was coming down in sheets and thunder rumbled through the sky. Just a summer storm, she told herself, nothing to worry about. Everything will be clean and fresh tomorrow and the roses in the garden will still have dewy drops of moisture on their petals. It will be perfect! Nothing will ruin the wedding. Nothing can.

Two

Shawna stared at her reflection as her mother adjusted the cream-colored lace of her veil. "How's that?" Doris McGuire asked as she met her daughter's gaze in the mirror.

"Fine, Mom. Really—" But Shawna's forehead was drawn into creases and her green eyes were dark with worry. *Where was Parker?*

Doris stepped back to take a better look and Shawna saw herself as her mother did. Ivory lace stood high on her throat, and creamy silk billowed softly from a tucked-in waist to a long train that was now slung over her arm. Wisps of honey-colored hair peeked from beneath her veil. The vision was complete, except for her clouded gaze. "Parker isn't here yet?" Shawna asked.

"Relax. Jake said he'd let us know the minute he arrived." She smoothed a crease from her dress and forced a smile.

"But he was supposed to meet with Reverend Smith half an hour ago."

Doris waved aside Shawna's worries. "Maybe he got caught in traffic. You know how bad it's been ever since the storm last night. Parker will be here. Just you wait. Before you know it, you'll be Mrs. Parker Harrison and Caribbean-bound."

"I hope so," Shawna said, telling herself not to worry. So Parker was a few minutes late; certainly that wasn't something to be alarmed about. Or was it? Parker had never been late once in the six weeks she'd known him.

Glancing through the window to the gray day beyond, Shawna watched the yellow ribbons woven into the white slats of the arbor in the church garden. They danced wildly over the roses of the outdoor altar as heavy purple clouds stole silently across the sky.

Doris checked her watch and sighed. "We still have time to move the ceremony inside," she said quietly. "I'm sure none of the guests would mind."

"No!" Shawna shook her head and her veil threatened to come loose. She heard the harsh sound of her voice and saw her mother stiffen. "Look, Mom, I'm sorry, I didn't mean to snap."

"It's okay—just the wedding-day jitters. But try to calm down," her mother suggested, touching her arm. "Parker will be here soon." But Doris's voice faltered and Shawna saw the concern etched in the corner of her mother's mouth.

"I hope you're right," she whispered, unconvinced. The first drops of rain fell from the sky and ran down the window panes. Glancing again out the window to the parking lot, Shawna hoped to see

Parker's red Jeep wheel into the lot. Instead, she saw Jake drive up, water splashing from under the wheels of his car as he ground to a stop.

"Where did Jake go?" she asked. "I thought he was in the rose garden . . ." Her voice drifted off as she watched her brother dash through the guests who were moving into the church.

"Shawna!" Jake's voice boomed through the door and he pounded on the wood panels. "Shawna!"

The ghost of fear swept over her.

"For God's sake, come in," Doris said, opening the door.

Jake burst into the room. His hair was wet, plastered to his head, his tuxedo was rumpled, and his face was colorless. "I just heard—there was an accident last night."

"An accident?" Shawna repeated, seeing the horror in his gaze. "No—"

"Parker and Brad were in a terrible crash. They weren't found until a few hours ago. Right now they're at Mercy Hospital—"

"There must be some mistake!" Shawna cried, her entire world falling apart. Parker couldn't be hurt! Just yesterday they were at the fair, laughing, kissing, touching . . .

"No mistake."

"Jake—" Doris reproached, but Jake was at Shawna's side, taking hold of her arm, as if he were afraid she would swoon.

"It's serious, Sis."

Disbelieving, Shawna pinned him with wide eyes. "If this is true—"

"Damn it, Shawna, do you think I'd run in here

with this kind of a story if I hadn't checked it out?" he asked, his voice cracking.

The last of her hopes fled and she clung to him, curling her fingers over his arm as fear grew in her heart. "Why didn't anyone tell me? I'm a doctor, for God's sake—"

"But not at Mercy Hospital. No one there knew who he was."

"But he's famous—"

"It didn't matter," Brad said soberly. His eyes told it all and for the first time Shawna realized that Parker, her beloved Parker, might die.

"Oh, my God," she whispered, wanting to fall to pieces, but not giving in to the horror that was coldly starting to grip her, wrenching at her insides. "I've got to go to him!"

"But you can't," her mother protested weakly. "Not now—"

"Of course I can!" Flinging off her veil, she gathered her skirts and ran to the side door of the church.

"Wait, Shawna!" Jake called after her, running to catch up. "I'll drive you—"

But she didn't listen. She found her purse with the car keys, jumped into her little hatchback, and plunged the keys into the ignition. The car roared to life. Shawna rammed it into gear and tore out of the parking lot, the car wheels screeching around the curves as she entered the highway. She drove wildly, her every thought centered on Parker as she prayed that he was still alive.

Jake hadn't said it, but it had been written in his eyes. *Parker might die!* "Please God, no," she whispered, her voice faltering, her chin thrust forward in determination. "You can't let him die! You can't!"

She shifted down, rounding a curve and nearly swerving out of her lane as the car climbed a steep street. Fir trees and church spires, skyscrapers and sharp ravines, a view of the Willamette River and the hazy mountains beyond were lost to her in a blur of rain-washed streets and fear.

Twice her car slid on the slick pavement but she finally drove into the parking lot of the hospital and ignored a sign reserving the first spot she saw for staff members. Her heart hammering with dread, she cut the engine, yanked on the brake and ran toward the glass doors, oblivious to the fact that her dress was dragging through mud-puddles and grime.

As she ran to the desk in the emergency room, she wiped the water from her face. "I need to see Parker Harrison," she said breathlessly to a calm-looking young woman at the desk. "I'm Dr. McGuire, Columbia Memorial Hospital." Flashing credentials in the surprised woman's face, she didn't wait for a response. "I'm also Mr. Harrison's personal physician. He was brought in here early this morning and I have to see him!"

"He's in surgery now—"

"Surgery!" Shawna said, incredulous. "Who's the doctor in charge?"

"Dr. Lowery."

"Then let me see Lowery." Shawna's eyes glittered with authority and determination, though inside she was dying. She knew her requests were unreasonable, against all hospital procedures, but she didn't care. Parker was in this hospital, somewhere, possibly fighting for his life, and come hell or high water, she was going to see him!

"You'll have to wait," the nurse said, glancing at

Shawna's wet hair, her bedraggled wedding dress, the fire in her gaze.

"I want to see him. Now."

"I'm sorry, Dr. McGuire. If you'd like, you could wait in the doctors' lounge and I'll tell Dr. Lowery you're here."

Seeing no other option, Shawna clamped her teeth together. "Then, please, tell me how serious he is. Exactly what are his injuries? How serious?"

"I can't give out that information."

Shawna didn't move. Her gaze was fixed on the smaller woman's face. "Then have someone who can give it out find me."

"If you'll wait."

Swallowing back the urge to shake information out of the young woman, Shawna exhaled a deep breath and tried to get a grip on her self-control. "Okay—but, please, send someone up to the lounge. I need to know about him, as his physician and as his fiancée."

The young nurse's face softened. "You were waiting for him, weren't you?" she asked quietly, as she glanced again at Shawna's soiled silk gown.

"Yes," Shawna admitted, her throat suddenly tight and tears springing to her eyes. She reached across the counter, took the nurse's hand in her own. "You understand—I have to see him."

"I'll send someone up as soon as I can," the girl promised.

"Thank you." Releasing her grip, Shawna suddenly felt the eyes of everyone in the waiting room boring into her back. For the first time she noticed the group of people assembled on the molded-plastic couches as they waited to be examined. Small children whined and cuddled against their mothers and older people, faces set and white, sat stiffly in the chairs, their eyes taking in Shawna's disheveled appearance.

Turning back to the young nurse, she forced her voice to remain steady. "Please, I want to know if there's any change in his condition." *Whatever that is,* she added silently.

"Will do, Dr. McGuire. The doctors' lounge is just to the left of the elevator on the second floor."

"Thank you," Shawna said, scooping up her skirts and squaring her shoulders as she started down the hall. The heels of her soaked satin pumps clicked on the tile floor.

"Shawna! Wait!" Jake's voice echoed through the corridor. In a few swift strides he was next to her, oblivious to the eyes of all the people in the waiting room. Still dressed in his tuxedo, his wet hair curling around his face, he looked as frantic as she felt. "What did you find out?" he asked softly.

"Not much. I'm on my way to the lounge on the second floor. Supposedly they'll send someone up to give me the news."

"If not, I'll check around—I've got connections here," Jake reminded her, glancing at all the pairs of interested eyes.

"You what?"

"Sometimes I consult here, at Mercy, in the psychiatric wing. I know quite a few of the staff. Come on," he urged, taking her elbow and propelling her toward the elevators. "You can change in the women's washroom on the second floor."

"Change?" she asked, realizing for the first time that he was carrying her smallest nylon suitcase, one of the suitcases she'd packed for her honeymoon. Numb inside, she took the suitcase from his outstretched hand. "Thanks," she murmured. "I owe you one."

"One of many. I'll add it to your list," he said, but the joke fell flat. "Look, Mom went through that," he gestured at the bag, "and thought you could find something more suitable than what you're wearing." Frowning, he touched her dirty gown.

The sympathy in Jake's eyes reached out to her and she felt suddenly weak. Her throat was hot, burning with tears she couldn't shed. "Oh, Jake. Why is this happening?" she asked, just as the elevator doors whispered open and they stepped inside.

"I wish I knew."

"I just want to know that Parker will be all right."

"I'll find out," he promised as the elevator groaned to a stop and Shawna stepped onto the second floor. Pushing a button on the control panel, Jake held the doors open and pointed down the hallway. "The lounge is right there, around the corner, and the washroom—I don't know where *that* is, but it must be nearby. I'll meet you back in the lounge as soon as I find Tom Handleman—he's usually in charge of ER—and then I'll be back to fill you in."

"Thanks," she whispered. The brackets around Jake's mouth deepened as he grimaced. "Let's just hope Parker and Brad are okay."

"They will be! They have to be!"

"I hope so. For your sake."

Then he was gone and Shawna, despite the fact that she was shaking from head to foot, found the washroom. Trying to calm herself, she sluiced cold water over her face and hardly recognized her reflection in the mirror over the sink. Two hours before she'd been a beaming bride, primping in front of a full-length mirror. Now, she looked as if she'd aged ten years. Eyes red, mouth surrounded by lines of strain, skin pale, she stripped off her wedding dress, unable to wear it another minute. Then she changed into a pair of white slacks, a cotton sweater, and a pair of running shoes, the clothes she had thought she would wear while holding hands with Parker and running along the gleaming white beach at Martinique.

Parker. Her heart wrenched painfully.

Quickly folding her dress as best she could and stuffing it into the little bag, she told herself to be strong and professional. Parker would be all right. He had to be.

Quickly, she found the lounge. With trembling hands, she poured herself a cup of coffee. Groups of doctors and nurses were clustered at round tables chattering, laughing, not seeming to care that Parker, her Parker, was somewhere in this labyrinthine building clinging to his very life. Forcing herself to remain calm, she took a chair in a corner near a planter filled with spiky leafed greenery. From there she could watch the door.

Doctors came and went, some with two days' growth of beard and red-rimmed eyes, others in crisply pressed lab coats and bright smiles. Each time the door opened, Shawna's gaze froze expectantly on the doorway, hoping that Jake would come barging into the room to tell her the entire nightmare was a hellish mistake; that Parker was fine; that nothing had changed; that later this afternoon they would step on a plane bound for white sand, hot sun, and aquamarine water . . .

"Come on, Jake," she whispered to herself, watching the clock as the second hand swept around the face, the minutes ticking by so slowly the waiting had become excruciating. She eavesdropped, listening to the conversations buzzing around her, dreading to overhear that Parker was dead, hoping to hear that his injuries were only superficial. But nothing was said.

Please, let him be all right! Please.

Somehow she finished her coffee and was shredding her cup when Jake pushed open the door and headed straight for her. Another young man was with him—tall and lean, with bushy salt and pepper hair, wire-rimmed glasses, and a sober expression. "Dr. McGuire?" he asked.

Bracing herself for the worst, Shawna met the young man's eyes.

"This is Tom Handleman, Shawna. He was just in ER with Parker," Jake explained.

"And?" she asked softly, her hands balling into fists.

"And he'll live," Tom said. "He was pinned in the car a long time, but his injuries weren't as bad as we'd expected."

"Thank God," she breathed, her voice breaking as relief drove aside her fears.

"He has several cracked ribs, a ruptured spleen, a concussion and a fractured patella, including torn cartilage and ripped ligaments. Besides which, there are facial lacerations and contusions—"

"And you don't think that's serious!" she cut in, the blood draining from her face.

Jake met her worried eyes. "Shawna, please, listen to him."

"I didn't say his condition wasn't serious," Tom replied. "But Mr. Harrison's injuries are no longer life-threatening."

"Concussion," she repeated, "ruptured spleen—"

"Right, but we've controlled the hemorrhaging and his condition has stabilized. As I said, his concussion wasn't as bad as Lowery and I had originally thought."

"No brain damage?" she asked.

"Not that we can tell. But he'll have to have knee surgery as soon as his body's well enough for the additional trauma."

She ran a shaking hand over her forehead. *Parker was going to be all right!* She felt weak with relief. "Can I see him?"

"Not yet. He's still in recovery," Tom said quietly. "But in a few hours, once he's conscious again— then you can see him."

"Was he conscious when he was brought in?"

"No." Dr. Handleman shook his head. "But we expect him to wake up as soon as the anesthetic wears off."

Jake placed his hand on Shawna's shoulder. "There's something else," he said quietly.

His grim expression and the fingers gripping her shoulder warned her. For the first time, she thought about the other man in Parker's car. "Brad?" she whispered, knowing for certain that Parker's star pupil and friend was dead.

"Brad Lomax was DOA," Tom said softly.

"Dead on arrival?" she repeated, the joy she'd felt so fleetingly stripped away.

"He was thrown from the car and his neck was broken."

"No!" she cried.

Jake's fingers tightened over her shoulders as she tried to stand and deny everything Tom was saying. She could see heads swing in her direction, eyes widen in interest as doctors at nearby tables heard her protest.

"I'm sorry," Tom said. "There was nothing we could do."

"But he was only twenty-two!"

"Shawna—" Jake's fingers relaxed.

Tears flooded her eyes. "I don't believe it!"

"You're a doctor, Miss McGuire," Tom pointed out, his eyes softening with sympathy. "You know as well as I do that these things happen. Not fair, I know, but just the way it is."

Sniffing back her tears, Shawna pushed Jake's restraining hands from her shoulders. Still grieving deep in her heart, she forced her professionalism to surface. "Thank you, Doctor," she murmured, extending her hand though part of her wanted to crumple into a miserable heap. As a doctor, she was used to dealing with death, but it was never easy, especially at a time like this, when the person who had lost his life was someone she'd known, someone Parker had loved.

Tom shook her hand. "I'll let you know when Mr. Harrison is awake and in his room. Why don't you go and rest for a couple of hours?"

"No—I, uh, I couldn't," she said.

"Your choice. Whatever I can do to help," he replied before turning and leaving the room.

"Oh, Jake," she said, feeling the security of her

brother's arm wrap around her as he led her from the lounge. "I just can't believe that Brad's gone—"

"It's hard, I know, but you've got to listen to me," he urged, handing her the nylon suitcase he'd picked up and helping her to the elevator. "What you'll have to do now is be strong, for Parker. When he wakes up and finds out that Brad is dead, he's going to feel guilty as hell—"

"But it wasn't his fault. It couldn't have been."

"I know," he whispered. "But Parker won't see the accident that way—not at first. The trauma of the accident combined with an overwhelming sense of guilt over Brad's death might be devastating for Parker. It would be for anyone." He squeezed her and offered a tight smile. "You'll have to be his rock, someone he can hold on to, and it won't be easy."

She met his gaze and determination shone in her eyes. "I'll do everything I can for him," she promised.

One side of Jake's mouth lifted upward. "I know it, Sis."

"The only thing that matters is that Parker gets well."

"And the two of you get married."

Her fingers clenched around the handle of her suitcase and she shook a wayward strand of hair from her eyes. "That's not even important right now," she said, steadfastly pushing all thoughts of her future with Parker aside. "I just have to see that he gets through this. And I will. No matter what!"

The next four hours were torture. She walked the halls of the hospital, trying to get rid of the nervous tension that twisted her stomach and made her glance at the clock every five minutes.

Jake had gone back to the church to explain what had happened to the guests and her parents, but she'd refused to give up her vigil.

"Dr. McGuire?"

Turning, she saw Dr. Handleman walking briskly to her.

"What's happened?" she asked. "I thought Parker was supposed to be put in a private room two hours ago."

"I know," he agreed, his face drawn, "but things changed. Unfortunately Mr. Harrison hasn't regained consciousness. We've done tests, the anesthesia has worn off, but he's still asleep."

Dread climbed up her spine. "Meaning?"

"Probably that he'll come to in the next twenty-four hours."

"And if he doesn't?" she asked, already knowing the answer, panic sending her heart slamming against her rib cage.

"Then we'll just have to wait."

"You're saying he's in a coma."

Tom pushed his glasses up his nose and frowned. "It looks that way."

"How long?"

"We can't guess."

"How long?" she repeated, jaw clenched, fear taking hold of her.

"Come on, *Dr.* McGuire, you understand what I'm talking about," he reminded her as gently as possible. "There's no way of knowing. Maybe just a few hours—"

"But maybe indefinitely," she finished, biting back the urge to scream.

"That's unlikely."

"But not out of the question."

He forced a tired smile. "Prolonged coma, especially after a particularly traumatic experience, is always a possibility."

"What about his knee?"

"It'll wait, but not too long. We can't let the bones start to knit improperly, otherwise we might have more problems than we already do."

"He's a tennis pro," she whispered.

"We'll take care of him," he said. "Now, if you want, you can see him. He's in room four-twelve."

"Thank you." Without a backward glance, she hurried to the elevator, hoping to stamp down the panic that tore at her. On the fourth floor, she strode briskly down the corridor, past rattling gurneys, clattering food trays, and the soft conversation of the nurses at their station as she made her way to Parker's room.

"Excuse me, miss," one nurse said as Shawna reached the door to room four-twelve. "But Mr. Harrison isn't allowed any visitors."

Shawna faced the younger woman and squared her shoulders, hoping to sound more authoritative than she felt. "I'm Dr. McGuire. I work at Columbia Memorial Hospital. Dr. Harrison is my patient and Dr. Handleman said I could wait for the patient to regain consciousness."

"It's all right," another nurse said. "I took the call from Dr. Handleman. Dr. McGuire has all privileges of a visiting physician."

"Thank you," Shawna said, entering the darkened room and seeing Parker's inert form on the bed. Draped in crisp, white sheets, lying flat on his back, with an IV tube running from his arm and a swath of bandages over his head, he was barely recognizable. "Oh, Parker," she whispered, throat clogged, eyes suddenly burning.

She watched the slow rise and fall of his chest, saw the washed-out color of his skin, the small cuts over his face, noticed the bandages surrounding his chest and kneecap, and she wondered if he'd ever be the same, wonderful man she'd known. "I love you," she vowed, twining her fingers in his.

Thinking of the day before, the hot sultry air, the brass ring, and the Gypsy woman's grim fortune, she closed her eyes.

You love him too much—you will lose him, the fortune-teller had predicted.

"Never," Shawna declared. Shivering, she took a chair near the bed, whispering words of endearment and telling herself that she would do everything in her power as a doctor and a woman to make him well.

Three

A breakfast cart rattled past the doorway and Shawna started, her eyelids flying open. She'd spent all day and night at Parker's beside, watching, waiting, and praying.

Now, as she rubbed the kinks from her neck and stretched her aching shoulder muscles, she looked down at Parker's motionless form, hardly believing that their life together had changed so drastically.

"Come on, Parker," she whispered, running gentle fingers across his forehead, silently hoping that his eyelids would flutter open. "You can do it."

A quiet cough caught her attention and she looked up to the doorway, where her brother lounged against the door frame. "How's it going?" Jake asked.

She lifted a shoulder. "About the same."

He raked his fingers through his hair and sighed. "How about if I buy you a cup of coffee?"

Shaking her head, Shawna glanced back at Parker. "I don't think I could—"

"Have you eaten anything since you've been here?"

"No, but—"

"That's right, no buts about it. I'm buying you breakfast. You're not doing Parker any good by starving yourself, are you, Doctor?"

"All right." Climbing reluctantly to her feet, she stretched again as she twisted open the blinds. The morning rays of late summer sun glimmered on the puddles outside. Deep in her heart, Shawna hoped the sunlight would wake Parker. She glanced back at him, her teeth sinking into her lower lip as she watched the steady rise and fall of his chest, noticed the bandage partially covering his head. But he didn't move.

"Come on," Jake said softly.

Without protest, she left the room. As she walked with Jake to the cafeteria, she was oblivious to the hospital routine: the nurses and orderlies carrying medication, the incessant pages from the intercom echoing down the corridors, the charts and files, and the ringing phones that normally sounded so familiar.

Jake pushed open the double doors to the dining room. Trays and silverware were clattering, and the smell of frying bacon, sizzling sausages, maple syrup, and coffee filled the air. Despite her despondency, Shawna's stomach grumbled and she let Jake buy her a platter of eggs, bacon, and toast.

Taking a seat at a scarred formica table, she sat across from her brother and tried to eat. But she couldn't help overhearing the gossip filtering her way. Two nurses at a nearby table were speaking in a loud whisper and Shawna could barely concentrate on her breakfast.

"It's a shame, really," a heavyset nurse was saying, clucking her tongue. "Parker Harrison of all people! You know, I used to watch his matches on TV."

"You and the rest of the country," her companion agreed.

Shawna's hands began to shake.

"And on his wedding day!" the first woman said. "And think about that boy and his family!"

"The boy?"

"Brad Lomax. DOA. There was nothing Lowery could do."

Shawna felt every muscle in her body tense. She was chewing a piece of toast, but it stuck in her throat.

"That explains the reporters crowded around the front door," the smaller woman replied.

"For sure. And that's not all of it. His fiancée is here, too. From what I hear she's a doctor over at Columbia Memorial. Been with him ever since the accident. She came charging over here in her wedding dress, demanding to see him."

"Poor thing."

Shawna dropped her fork and her fists curled in anger. *How dare they gossip about Parker!*

"Right. And now he's comatose. No telling when he'll wake up."

"Or if."

Shawna's shoulders stiffened and she was about to say something, but Jake held up his hand and shook his head. "Don't bother," he suggested. "It's just small talk."

"About Parker and me!"

"He's a famous guy. So was Brad Lomax. Loosen up, Shawna, you've heard hospital gossip before."

"Not about Parker," she muttered, her appetite waning again as she managed to control her temper. The two nurses carried their trays back to the counter and Shawna tried to relax. Of course Parker's accident had created a stir and people were only people. Jake was right. She had to expect curiosity and rumors.

"I know this is hard. But it's not going to get much better, at least for a while." He finished his stack of pancakes and pushed his plate to one side. "You may as well know that the reporters have already started calling. There were several recordings on your phone machine this morning."

"You were at my apartment?"

"I took back your bag and I gave the wedding dress to Mom. She's going to have it cleaned, but isn't sure that it will look the same."

"It doesn't matter," Shawna said. She wondered if she'd ever wear the gown again. "How're Mom and Dad?"

"They're worried about you and Parker."

"I'll bet," she whispered, grateful for her parents and their strength. Whereas Parker was strong because he'd grown up alone, never knowing his parents, Shawna had gotten her strength from the support and security of her family.

"Mom's decided to keep a low profile."

"And Dad?"

"He wants to tear down the walls of this hospital."

"It figures."

"But Mom has convinced him that if you need them, you'll call."

"Or you'll tell them, if I don't," Shawna guessed.

Smiling slightly, he said. "They're just trying to

give you some space—but you might want to call them."

"I will. Later. After Parker wakes up."

Jake raised one brow skeptically, but if he had any doubts, he kept them to himself. "Okay, I'll give them the message."

She quit pretending interest in her food and picked up her tray. She'd been away from Parker for nearly half an hour and she had to get back.

"There's something you should remember," Jake said as they made their way through the tightly packed formica tables, setting their trays on the counter.

"And what's that?"

"When you leave the hospital, you might want to go out a back entrance, unless you're up to answering a lot of personal questions from reporters."

"I understand. Thanks for the warning."

She turned toward the elevator, but Jake caught her elbow.

"There is one other thing. Brad Lomax's funeral is the day after tomorrow. Mom already arranged to send a spray of flowers from you and Parker."

Shawna winced at the mention of Brad's name. His death was still difficult to accept. And then there was the matter of Parker and how he would feel when he found out what had happened to his protégé. "Mom's an angel," Shawna decided, "but I think I'd better put in an appearance."

"The funeral's for family only," Jake told her. "Don't think about it."

Relieved, Shawna said, "I'll try not to. I'll see you later." Waving, she dashed to the stairwell, unable to wait for the elevator. She had to get back to

Parker and make sure she was the one who broke the news.

Parker felt as if his head would explode. Slowly he opened an eye, ignoring the pain that shot through his brain. He tried to lift a hand to his head, but his cramped muscles wouldn't move and his struggling fingers felt nothing save cold metal bars.

Where am I? he wondered, trying to focus. There was a bad taste in his mouth and pain ripped up one side of his body and down the other. His throat worked, but no sound escaped.

"He's waking up!" a woman whispered, her voice heavy with relief. The voice was vaguely familiar, but he couldn't place it. "Call Dr. Handleman or Dr. Lowery! Tell them Parker Harrison is waking up!"

What the hell for? And who are Lowery and Handleman? Doctors? Is that what she said?

"Parker? Can you hear me? Parker, love?"

He blinked rapidly, focusing on the face pressed close to his. It was a beautiful face, with even features, pink-tinged cheeks, and worried green eyes. Long, slightly wavy honey-colored hair fell over her shoulders to brush against his neck.

"Oh, God, I'm so glad you're awake," she said, her voice thick with emotion. Tears starred her lashes and for the first time he noticed the small lines of strain near her mouth and the hollows of her cheeks.

She's crying! This beautiful young woman was actually shedding tears. He was amazed as he watched her tears drizzle down her cheeks and one by one drop onto the bed sheets. She was crying for him! But why?

Her hands were on his shoulders and she buried her face into the crook of his neck. Her tenderness seemed right, somehow, but for the life of him, he couldn't understand why. "I've been so worried! It's been three days! Thank God, you're back!"

His gaze darted around the small room, to the television, the rails on the bed, the dripping IV hanging over his head, and the baskets and baskets of flowers sitting on every available space in the room. It slowly dawned on him that he was in a hospital. The pain in his head wasn't imagined, this wasn't all a bad dream. Somehow he'd landed in a hospital bed, completely immobilized!

"Good morning, Mr. Harrison!" a gruff male voice called.

The woman straightened and quickly brushed aside her tears.

Shifting his gaze, Parker saw a man he didn't recognize walk up to the bed and smile down at him. A doctor. Dressed in a white lab coat, with an identification tag that Parker couldn't make out, the man stared down at Parker from behind thick, wire-framed glasses. Taking Parker's wrist in one hand, he glanced at his watch. "I'm Dr. Handleman. You're a patient here in Mercy Hospital and have been for the past three days."

Three days? What in God's name was this man talking about? Partial images, horrible and vague, teased his mind, though he couldn't remember what they meant.

Drawing his brows together in concentration, Parker tried to think, strained to remember, but his entire life was a blur of disjointed pieces that were colorless and dreamlike. He had absolutely no idea who these people were or why he was here.

"You're a very lucky man," the doctor continued, releasing his wrist. "Not many people could have survived that accident."

Parker blinked, trying to find his voice. "Accident?" he rasped, the sound of his own voice unfamiliar and raw.

"You don't remember?" The doctor's expression clouded.

"Wh-what am I doing here?" Parker whispered hoarsely. His eyes traveled past the doctor to the woman. She was leaning against the wall, as if for support. Wearing a white lab coat and a stethoscope, she had to be a member of the staff. *So why the tears?* "Who are you?" he asked, his bruised face clouding as he tried to concentrate. He heard her muted protest and saw the slump of her shoulders. "Do I know you?"

Four

Shawna's heart nearly stopped. "Parker?" she whispered, struggling to keep her voice steady as she took his bandaged hand in hers. "Don't you remember me?"

His gaze skated over her face and he squinted, as if trying to remember something hazy, but no flash of recognition flickered in his eyes.

"I'm Shawna," she said slowly, hoping to hide the tremble of her lips. "Shawna McGuire."

"A doctor?" he guessed, and Shawna wanted to die.

"Yes—but more than that."

Tom Handleman caught her eye, warning her not to push Parker too hard, but Shawna ignored him. This was important. Parker had to remember! He couldn't forget—not about the love they'd shared, the way they had felt and cared about each other.

"We were supposed to be married," she said quietly, watching his thick brows pull together in consternation. "The day after your accident, at Pioneer Church, in the rose arbor . . . I waited for you."

He didn't say a word, just stared at her as if she were a complete stranger.

"That's enough for now," Tom Handleman said, stepping closer to the bed, snapping on his penlight, trying to end the emotional scene. "Let's take a look at you, Mr. Harrison."

But before Tom could shine his penlight into Parker's eyes, Parker grabbed the doctor's wrist. The crisp sheets slid from one side of the bed, exposing his bare leg and the bandages, still streaked with dried blood. "What the hell's going on?" he demanded, his voice gruff and nearly unrecognizable. "What happened to me? What's she talking about?" He glanced back to Shawna. "What marriage? I've never even been engaged—" Then his eyes dropped to Shawna's left hand and the winking diamond on her ring finger.

"Mr. Harrison, please—"

"Just what the hell happened to me?" Parker repeated, trying to sit up, only to blanch in pain.

"Parker, please," Shawna whispered, restraining him with her hands. She could feel his shoulder muscles, hard and coiled, flexing as he attempted to sit upright. "Just calm down. We'll straighten this all out. You'll remember, I promise." But she had to fight the catch in her throat and her professionalism drained away from her. She couldn't be cool or detached with Parker. "Dr. Handleman's your physician."

"I don't *know* any Handleman. Where's Jack Pederson?"

"Who?" Handleman asked, writing quickly on Parker's chart.

Shawna glanced nervously to the doctor. "Jack was Parker's trainer."

"Was?" Parker repeated, his features taut from pain and the effort of trying to remember those tiny pieces of his past that teased him, rising just to the surface of his mind only to sink deeper into murky oblivion. "Was?"

"That was a couple of years ago," Shawna said quickly.

"What're you talking about? Just last Saturday, Jack and I—" But he didn't finish and his features slackened suddenly as he turned bewildered blue eyes on Handleman. "No, it wasn't Saturday," he whispered, running one hand through his hair and feeling, for the first time, the bandages surrounding his head. Involuntarily his jaw tightened. "Maybe you'd better fill me in," he said, dropping his hand and pinning Tom Handleman with his gaze. "What the hell happened to me?"

"You were in an accident. Several days ago."

Parker closed his eyes, trying vainly to remember.

"From what the police tell me, a truck swerved into your lane, your Jeep crashed through the guard rail, and you were pinned inside the vehicle for several hours. They brought you in here, we performed surgery, and you've been unconscious ever since."

Parker seemed about to protest, but didn't. Instead he listened in stony silence as Tom described his injuries and prognosis.

"So, now that you're awake and the swelling in your leg has gone down, we'll do surgery on that knee. It will all take a little time. You'll be in physical therapy for awhile, then you'll be good as new—or almost."

"How long is 'awhile'?"

"That depends upon you and how everything heals."

"Just give me an educated guess."

Handleman crossed his arms over his chest, folding Parker's chart against his lab coat. "I'll be straight with you, Mr. Harrison."

"I'd appreciate that—and call me Parker."

"Fair enough, Parker. It could take anywhere from three months to a year of physical therapy before you can play tennis again. But, if you set your mind to it, work hard, I'll bet you'll be walking without crutches in six months."

Parker's jaw was rock hard and his eyes, clouded, moved from Tom's face to Shawna's. "Okay. That answers one question. Now, tell me about the driver of the truck—is he okay?"

"Not a scratch," Tom replied. "You missed him completely, even though he was all over the road. He was too drunk to report the accident."

A muscle jerked in Parker's jaw as he tried to remember. Horrifying images taunted him, but he couldn't quite make them out. Nonetheless his heart began to beat unsteadily and his hands, beneath bandages, had started to sweat. "There's something else, though," he said, rubbing his eyes. "Something—I can't remember. Something . . . important." *God, what is it?*

Shawna cleared her throat. Though she tried to appear calm, Parker read the hint of panic in the way she glanced at Handleman and toyed with the strand of pearls at her neck. "Maybe that's enough for you right now," she said.

"You know something, both of you. Something you're keeping from me."

Shawna, feeling the urge to protect him, to lie if she had to, to do anything to keep him from the horrid truth, touched his arm. "Just rest now."

"Is that your professional advice?" Parker asked. "Or are you trying to put me off?"

"Professional," Tom said, quickly, rescuing Shawna. "A nurse will be in to take your temperature and order you some lunch— "

"Wait a minute." Parker's voice was stern. "Something's wrong here, I can feel it. There's something you're not telling me about the accident." *What the hell is it?* Then he knew. "Someone else was involved," he said flatly. "Who?"

Shawna's shoulders stiffened a bit and her fingers found his on the cold metal railing.

Handleman offered a professional smile. "Right now all you have to worry about is—"

Parker sat bolt upright, tearing the IV tubing from the rail of the bed and ignoring the jab of pain in his knee. He kicked off the sheets and tried to climb out of bed. "What I have to worry about is who was with me. Where is he—or she?" Fire flared in his eyes as Handleman tried to restrain him. "I have the right to know!"

"Whoa—Parker, settle down," Handleman said.

"Who, dammit!"

"Brad Lomax," Shawna whispered, unable to meet the confused torture in his eyes.

"Lomax?"

"He was in the car with you. He drank too much at our wedding rehearsal dinner and you were taking him home."

"But I don't remember—" He swallowed then, his eyes clouding. Somewhere deep in his mind he remembered the squeal of tires, the shatter of glass, felt his muscles wrench as he jerked hard on the steering wheel, heard a terrifying scream. "Oh, God," he rasped. "Who is he?"

"A tennis pro. Your student." Shawna felt her eyes grow moist as she watched the skin over his cheekbones turn white and taut.

"I was driving," he said slowly, as if measuring each agonizing word. "Lomax. How is he?"

"I'm afraid he didn't make it," Tom replied, exchanging glances with Shawna.

"He was killed in the wreck?" Parker's voice was sharp and fierce with self-loathing. "I killed him?"

"It was an accident," Shawna said quickly. "An unfortunate one—his seat belt malfunctioned and he was pinned under the Jeep."

Parker blinked several times, then lay back on the pillows as he struggled with his past. This couldn't be happening—he didn't even know these people! Maybe if he just went back to sleep he'd wake up and this hellish dream with the beautiful woman and clouded jags of memory would go away. "Does Lomax have any family?"

Just you, Shawna thought, but shook her head. "Only an uncle and a couple of cousins, I think."

"I think you'd better get some rest now," Tom advised, motioning to a nurse standing by the door. "I want Mr. Harrison sedated—"

"No!" Parker's eyes flew open.

"This has all been such a shock—"

"I can handle it," Parker said tightly, his face grim and stern. "No sedative, no pain killers. Got it?"

"But—"

"Got it?" he repeated, some of his old fire returning. "And don't try slipping anything into this!" He lifted his fist with the IV tubes attached.

Handleman's mouth became a thin white line. "Lie back down, Mr. Harrison," he said sternly, waiting until Parker reluctantly obeyed. "Now, it's my job to see that you're taken care of—that you rest. But I'll need your help. Either you contain yourself or I'll have the nurse sedate you."

Muscles rigid, eyes bright with repressed fury, Parker stared at the ceiling.

"Good. Just let me know if you change your mind about the sedatives or the pain killers. Now, Shawna, I think Mr. Harrison needs his rest."

"Wait a minute," Parker insisted, reaching for Shawna's hand again. "I want to talk to you. Alone." His gaze drilled past Handleman's thick glasses, and fortunately, the doctor got the message. With a nod of his head, he tucked his clipboard under his arm, left the room, and closed the door.

"Tell me," he said, forcing himself to be calm, though his fingers clenched tightly over hers.

"About what?"

"Everything."

Shawna sighed and sagged against the bed. How could she begin to explain the whirlwind fantasy that had been their relationship? How could she recount how Parker had seen the potential in a streetwise juvenile delinquent and had turned him into one of the finest young tennis players in the nation—a boy who had become a younger brother to him?

"Tell me," he insisted, hungry for knowledge of himself.

"First things first. What do you remember?"

"Not enough!" he said sharply, then took a deep breath. "Not nearly enough."

"I'll tell you what I can," she said, "but you've got to promise to stay calm."

"I don't know if that's possible," he admitted.

"Then we haven't got a deal, have we?"

Swearing under his breath, he forced a grin he obviously didn't feel. "Okay," he said. "Deal."

"Good."

"Something tells me I should remember you."

"Most definitely," she agreed, feeling better than she had since the accident and grinning as she blinked back tears. Then, as all her bravado crumbled, she touched him gently on his forehead. "Oh, Parker, I've missed you—God, how I've missed you." Without thinking, she leaned forward and kissed him, brushing her lips suggestively over his and tasting the salt from her own tears.

But Parker didn't respond, just stared at her with perplexed blue eyes.

Shawna cleared her throat. "Fortunately, that part—the loneliness—is over now," she said, quickly sniffing back her tears. "And once you're out of here, we'll get married, and go to the Bahamas, have a ton of children, and live happily ever after!"

"Hey, whoa. Slow down," he whispered. Rubbing one hand over his jaw, he said, "Tell me about Brad Lomax."

Shawna realized he wouldn't give up. Though she felt the urge to protect him, she decided he had to face the truth sooner or later. She wanted to soften the blow, but she had to be honest with him. "Brad Lomax," she said uneasily, "was a hellion, and he was a terror on the tennis courts, and you saw something in him. You recognized his raw talent and took him under your wing. You and he were very close," she admitted, seeing the pain in his eyes. "You knew him a lot longer than you've known me."

"How close?" Parker asked, his voice low.

"You were his mentor—kind of a big brother. He looked up to you. That night, the night of the accident, he'd had too much to drink and wanted to talk to you. You offered to take him home."

A muscle worked in his jaw. "Why did he want to talk to me?"

Shawna lifted a shoulder. "I don't know. No one does. I suppose now that no one ever will."

"I killed him," Parker said quietly.

"No, Parker. It was an accident!" she said vehemently.

"How old was he?"

"Don't do this to yourself."

"How old was he?" His eyes drilled into hers.

"Twenty-two," she whispered.

"Oh, God." With a shudder, he closed his eyes. "I should have been the one who died, you know."

Shawna resisted the overpowering urge to cradle his head to her breast and comfort him. The torture twisting his features cut her to the bone. "Don't do this, Parker. It's not fair."

Parker stared up at her with simmering blue eyes. His expression was a mixture of anguish and awe, and his hand reached upward, his fingers slipping beneath her hair to caress her nape.

She trembled at his touch, saw the torment in his gaze.

"I don't remember where I met you. Or how. Or

even who you are," he admitted, his voice husky, the lines near his mouth softening as he stared up at her. "But I do know that I'm one lucky son of a bitch if you were planning to marry me."

"Am—as in present tense," she corrected, her throat hot with unshed tears. "I still intend to march down the aisle with you, Parker Harrison, whether you're in a cast, on crutches, or in a wheelchair."

She felt his fingers flex as he drew her head to his, and he hesitated only slightly before touching his lips to hers. "I will remember you," he promised, eyes dusky blue. "No matter what it takes!"

Her heart soared. All they needed was a little time!

Tom Handleman, his expression stern behind his wire-rimmed glasses, poked his head into the room. "Doctor?"

"That's my cue," Shawna whispered, brushing her lips against Parker's hair. "I'll be back."

"I'm counting on it."

She forced herself out of the room, feeling more lighthearted than she had in days. So what if Parker didn't remember her? What did it matter that he had a slight case of amnesia? The important consideration was his health, and physically he seemed to be gaining strength. Although mentally he still faced some tough hurdles, she was confident that with her help, Parker would surmount any obstacle fate cast his way. It was only a matter of time before he was back on his feet again and they could take up where they'd left off.

Jake was waiting for her in the hallway. Slouched into one of the waiting-room chairs, his tie askew, his shirtsleeves rolled over his forearms, he groaned as he stretched to his feet and fell into step with her. "Good news," he guessed, a wide grin spreading across his beard-stubbled jaw.

"The best!" Shawna couldn't contain herself. "He's awake!"

"About time!" Jake winked at her. "So, when's the wedding?"

Shawna chuckled. "I think Parker and I have a few bridges to cross first."

"Meaning Brad's death?"

"For one," she said, linking her arm through her brother's and pushing the elevator button. "You can buy me lunch and I'll explain about the rest of them."

"There's more?"

"A lot more," she said as they squeezed into the crowded elevator and she lowered her voice. "He doesn't remember me—or much else for that matter."

Jake let out a long, low whistle.

"You're used to dealing with this, aren't you, in your practice?" she asked eagerly.

"I've seen a couple of cases."

"Then maybe you can work with him."

"Maybe," he said, his gray eyes growing thoughtful.

As the elevator opened at the hallway near the cafeteria, Shawna sent him a teasing glance, "Well, don't trip all over yourself to help."

"I'll do what I can," he said, massaging his neck muscles. "Unfortunately, you'll have to be patient, and that's not your strong suit."

"Patient?"

"You know as well as I do that amnesia can be tricky. He may remember everything tomorrow, or . . ."

"Or it may take weeks," she said with a sigh. "I can't even think about that. Not now. I'm just thanking my lucky stars that he's alive and he'll be all right."

Maybe, Jake thought, steering Shawna down the stainless steel counter and past cream pies, jello, and fruit salad. Only time would tell.

Parker tried to roll off the bed, but a sharp pain in his knee and the IV tube stuck into his hand kept him flat on his back. He had a restless urge to get up, walk out of the hospital, and catch hold of the rest of his life—wherever it was.

He knew who he was. He could remember some things very clearly—the death of his parents in a boating accident, the brilliance of a trophy glinting gold in the sun. But try as he might, he couldn't conjure up Brad Lomax's face to save his soul.

And this Shawna woman with her honey-gold hair, soft lips, and intense green eyes. She was a doctor and they'd planned to be married? That didn't seem to fit. Nor did her description of his being some heroic do-gooder who had saved a boy from self-destruction while molding him into a tennis star.

No, her idealistic views of his life didn't make a helluva lot of sense. He remembered winning, playing to the crowd, enjoying being the best; he'd been ruthless and unerring on the court—the "ice man," incapable of emotion.

And yet she seemed to think him some sort of modern-day good Samaritan. No way!

Struggling for the memories locked just under the surface of his consciousness, he closed his eyes and clenched his fists in frustration. Why couldn't he remember? Why?

"Mr. Harrison?"

He opened one eye, then the other. A small nurse was standing just inside the door.

"Glad you're back with us," she said, rolling in a clattering tray of food—if that's what you'd call the unappetizing gray potatoes-and-gravy dish she set in front of him. "Can I get you anything else?"

"Nothing," he replied testily, his thoughts returning to the beautiful doctor and the boy whose face he couldn't remember. *I don't want anything but my past.* Sighing, the nurse left.

Parker shoved the tray angrily aside and closed his eyes, willing himself to remember, concentrating on that dark void that was his past. Shawna. Had he known her? How? Had he really planned to marry her?

Sleep overcame him in warm waves and bits of memory played with his mind. Dreaming, he saw himself dancing with a gorgeous woman in a mist-cloaked rose garden. Her face was veiled and she was dressed in ivory silk and lace, he in a stiff tuxedo. Her scent and laughter engulfed him as they stopped dancing to sip from crystal glasses of champagne. Sweeping her into his arms again, he spilled champagne on the front of her gown and she tossed back her head but her veil stayed in place, blocking his view of her eyes as he licked the frothy bubbles from the beaded lace covering her throat.

"I love you," she vowed, sighing. "Forever."

"And I love you."

Light-headed from the drink and the nearness of her, he captured her lips with his, tasting cool, effervescent wine on her warm lips. Her fingers toyed his bow tie, loosening it from his neck, teasing him, and he caught a glimpse of her dimpled smile before she slipped away from him. He tried to call out to her, but he didn't know her name and his voice was muted. Desperate not to lose her, he grasped at her dress but clutched only air. She was floating away from him, her face still a guarded mystery. . . .

Parker's eyes flew open and he took in a swift breath. His hand was clenched, but empty. The dream had been so real, so lifelike, as if he'd been in that garden with that beautiful woman. But now, in his darkened hospital room, he wondered if the dream had been part of his memory or only something he wanted so fervently he'd created the image.

Had the woman been Shawna McGuire?

Dear God, he hoped so. She was, without a doubt, the most intriguing woman he'd ever met.

The next evening, in her office at Columbia Memorial Hospital on the east side of the Willamette River, Shawna leaned back in her chair until it creaked in protest. Unpinning her hair, letting it fall past her shoulders in a shimmering gold curtain, she closed her eyes and imagined that Parker's memory was restored and they were getting married, just as they planned.

"Soon," she told herself as she stretched and flipped through the pages of her appointment book.

Because she couldn't stand the idea of spending hour upon hour with nothing to do, she had rescheduled her vacation—the time she had meant to use on her honeymoon—and today had been her first full day of work since the accident. She was dead tired. The digital clock on her desk blinked the time. It was eight-fifteen, and she hadn't eaten since breakfast.

She'd finished her rounds early, dictated patient

diagnoses into the tiny black machine at her desk, answered some correspondence and phone calls, and somehow managed to talk to the amnesia specialist on staff at Columbia Memorial. Her ears still rang with his advice.

"Amnesia's not easy to predict," Pat Barrington had replied to her questions about Parker. A kindly neurosurgeon with a flushed red face and horn-rimmed glasses, he'd told Shawna nothing she hadn't really already known. "Parker's obviously reacting to the trauma, remembering nothing of the accident or the events leading up to it," Barrington had said, punching the call button for the elevator.

"So why doesn't he remember Brad Lomax or me?"

"Because you're both part of it, really. The accident occurred right after the rehearsal dinner. Subconsciously, he's denying everything leading up to the accident—even your engagement. Give him time, Shawna. He's not likely to forget you," Barrington had advised, clapping Shawna on her back.

Now, as Shawna leaned back in her chair, she sighed and stared out the window into the dark September night. "Time," she whispered. Was it her friend or enemy?

Five

Two weeks later, Shawna sipped from her teacup and stared through the kitchen window of her apartment at the late afternoon sky. Parker's condition hadn't changed, except that the surgery on his knee had been a success. He was already working in physical therapy to regain use of his leg, but his mind, as far as Shawna and the wedding were concerned, was a complete blank. Though Shawna visited him each day, hoping to help him break through the foggy wall surrounding him, he stared at her without a flicker of the warmth she'd always felt in his gaze.

Now, as she dashed the dregs of her tea into the sink, she decided she couldn't wait any longer. Somehow, she had to jog his memory. She ached to touch him again, feel his arms around her, have him talk to her as if she weren't a total stranger.

"You're losing it, McGuire," she told herself as she glanced around her kitchen. Usually bright and neat, the room was suffering badly from neglect. Dishes were stacked in the sink, the floor was dull, and there were half-filled boxes scattered on the counters and floor.

Before the wedding she'd packed most of her things, but now she'd lost all interest in moving from the cozy little one-bedroom apartment she'd called home for several years. Nonetheless, she had given her notice and would have to move at the end of the month.

Rather than consider the chore of moving, she stuffed two packets of snapshots into her purse and found her coat. Then, knowing she was gambling with her future, she grabbed her umbrella and dashed through the front door of her apartment.

Outside, the weather was gray and gloomy. Rain drizzled from the sky, ran in the gutters of the old turn-of-the-century building, and caught on the broad leaves of the rhododendron and azaleas flanking the cement paths.

"Dr. McGuire!" a crackly voice accosted her. "Wait up!"

Shawna glanced over her shoulder. Mrs. Swenson, her landlady, clad in a bright yellow raincoat, was walking briskly in her direction. Knowing what was to come, Shawna managed a smile she didn't feel. "Hi, Mrs. Swenson."

"I know you're on your way out," Mrs. Swenson announced, peering into the bushes near Shawna's front door and spying the lurking shadow of Maestro, Shawna's yellow tabby near the steps. Adjusting her plastic rain bonnet, Mrs. Swenson pursed her lips and peered up at Shawna with faded gold eyes. "But I thought we'd better talk about your apartment. I know about your troubles with Mr. Harrison and it's a darned shame, that's what it is—but I've got tenants who've planned to lease your place in about two weeks."

"I know, I know," Shawna said. If her life hadn't been shattered by the accident, she would already have moved into Parker's house on the Willamette River. But, of course, the accident had taken care of that. "Things just haven't exactly fallen into place."

"I know, I know," Mrs. Swenson said kindly, still glancing at the cat. "But, be that as it may, the Levertons plan to start moving in the weekend after next and your lease is up. Then there's the matter of having the place painted, the drapes cleaned, and whatnot. I hate to be pushy . . . but I really don't have much choice."

"I understand," Shawna admitted, thinking over her options for the dozenth time. "And I'll be out by Friday night. I promise."

"That's only four days away," Mrs. Swenson pointed out, her wrinkled face puckering pensively.

"I've already started packing." Well, not really, but she did have some things in boxes, things she'd stored when she and Parker had started making wedding plans. "I can store my things with my folks and live either with them or with Jake," she said. The truth of the matter was, deep down, she still intended to move into Parker's place, with or without a wedding ring. In the past few weeks since the accident, she'd discovered just how much she loved him, and that a certificate of marriage wasn't as important as being with him.

"And what're you planning to do about that?" the old woman asked, shaking a gnarled finger at Maestro as he nimbly jumped onto the window ledge. With his tail flicking anxiously, he glared in through the window to the cage where Mrs. Swenson's yellow parakeet ruffled his feathers and chirped loudly enough to be heard through the glass.

"He's not really mine—"

"You've been feeding him, haven't you?"

"Well, yes. But he just strayed—"

"Two years ago," Mrs. Swenson interjected. "And if he had his way my little Pickles would have been his dinner time and time again."

"I'll take him with me."

"Good. Saves me a trip to the animal shelter," Mrs. Swenson said. Shawna seriously doubted the old woman had the heart to do anything more dastardly than give Maestro a saucer of milk—probably warmed in the microwave. Though outwardly a curmudgeon, Myrna Swenson had a heart of gold buried beneath a crusty layer of complaining.

"I'll tell Eva Leverton she can start packing."

"Good!" Shawna climbed into her car and watched as Mrs. Swenson cooed to the bird in the window. She flicked on the engine, smothered a smile, and muttered, "Pickles is a dumb name for a bird!" Then slamming the car into gear, she drove away from the apartment complex.

More determined than ever to help Parker regain his memory, Shawna wheeled across the Ross Island bridge and up the steep grade of the west hills to Mercy Hospital.

Today Parker would remember her, she decided with a determined smile as she pulled on the emergency brake and threw open the car door. Sidestepping puddles of rain water, she hurried inside the old concrete and glass of Mercy Hospital.

She heard Parker before she saw him. Just as the elevator doors parted on the fourth floor, Parker's voice rang down the gray-carpeted hallway.

"Hey, watch out, you're killing me!" he barked and Shawna smothered a grin. One of the first signs of patient improvement was general irritability, and Parker sounded as if he was irritable in spades.

"Good morning," Shawna said, cautiously poking her head into the room.

"What's good about it?" Parker grumbled.

"I see our patient is improving," she commented to the orderly trying to adjust the bed.

"Not his temperament," the orderly confided.

"I heard that," Parker said, but couldn't help flashing Shawna a boyish grin—the same crooked grin she'd grown to love. Her heart did a stupid little leap, the way it always did when he rained his famous smile on her.

"Be kind, Parker," she warned, lifting some wilting roses from a ceramic vase and dropping the wet flowers into a nearby trash basket. "Otherwise he might tell the people in physical therapy to give you the 'torture treatment,' and I've heard it can be murder."

"Humph." He laughed despite his ill humor and the orderly ducked gratefully out the door.

"You're not making any friends here, you know," she said, sitting on the end of his bed and leaning back to study him. Her honey-colored hair fell loose behind her shoulders, and a small smile played on her lips.

"Am I supposed to be?"

"If you don't want your breakfast served cold, your temperature to be taken at four A.M., or your T.V. cable to be mysteriously tampered with."

"I'd pay someone to do it," Parker muttered. "Then maybe I wouldn't have to watch any more of that." He nodded in the direction of the overhead television. On the small screen, a wavy-haired reporter with a bright smile was sitting behind a huge desk while discussing the worldwide ranking of America's tennis professionals.

"—and the tennis world is still reeling from the unfortunate death of Brad Lomax, perhaps the brightest star in professional tennis since his mentor, Parker Harrison's, meteoric burst onto the circuit in the midseventies."

A picture of Brad, one arm draped affectionately over Parker's broad shoulders, the other hand holding a winking brass trophy triumphantly overhead, was flashed onto the screen. Brad's dark hair was plastered to his head, sweat dripped down his face, and a fluffy white towel was slung around his neck. Parker, his chestnut hair glinting in the sun, his face tanned and unlined, his eyes shining with pride, stood beside his protégé.

Now, as she watched, Shawna's stomach tightened. Parker lay still, his face taut and white as the newscaster continued. *"Lomax, whose off-court escapades were as famous as his blistering serves, was killed just over two weeks ago when the vehicle Parker Harrison was driving swerved off the road and crashed down a hundred-foot embankment.*

"Harrison is still reported in stable condition, though there're rumors that he has no memory of the near-collision with a moving van which resulted in the—"

Ashen-faced, Shawna snapped the television off. "I don't know why you watch that stuff!"

Parker didn't answer, just glanced out the window to the rain-soaked day and the gloomy fir boughs visible through his fourth-floor window. "I'm just trying to figure out who I am."

"And I've told you—"

"But I don't want the romanticized version—just the facts," he said, his gaze swinging back to hers. "I want to remember—for myself. I want to remember *you*."

"You will. I promise," she whispered.

He sighed in frustration, but touched her hand, his fingers covering hers. "For the past week people have been streaming in here—people I should know and don't. There have been friends, reporters, doctors, and even the mayor, for heaven's sake! They ask questions, wish me well, tell me to take it easy, and all the time I'm thinking, 'who the hell are you?' "

"Parker—" Leaning forward, she touched his cheek, hoping to break through the damming wall blocking his memory.

"Don't tell me to be patient," he said sharply, but his eyes were still warm as they searched her face. "Just take one look around this room, for crying out loud!" Everywhere there were piles of cards and letters, huge baskets of fruit, tins of cookies and vases of heavy-blossomed, fragrant flowers. "Who *are* these people?" he asked, utterly perplexed.

Shawna wanted to cry. "People who care, Parker," she said, her voice rough as her hands covered his, feeling the warmth of his palms against her skin. She treasured the comfort she felt as his fingers grazed her cheekbones. "People who care about us."

He swore under his breath. "And I can't remember half of them. Here I am with enough flowers to cover all the floats in the Rose Parade and enough damned fruit and banana bread to feed all the starving people in the world—"

"You're exaggerating," she charged.

"Well, maybe just a little," he admitted, his lips twisting into a wry grin.

"A lot!"

"Okay, a lot."

She stroked his brow, hoping to ease the furrows in his forehead. "Unfortunately neither of us can undo what's happened. Don't you think that I would change things if I could? That I would push back the hands of the clock so that I could have you back—all of you." She swallowed against a huge lump forming in her throat.

He rested his forehead against hers. His gaze took in every soft angle of her face, the way her lashes swept over her eyes, the tiny lines of concern etching the ivory-colored skin of her forehead, the feel of her breath, warm and enticing against his face. Old emotions, cloaked in that black recess of the past, stirred, but refused to emerge. "Oh, why can't I remember you?" His voice was so filled with torment and longing, she buried her face in his shoulder and twisted her fingers in the folds of his sheets.

"Try," she pleaded.

"I have—over and over again." His eyes were glazed as he stroked her chin. "If you believe anything, believe that I want to remember you . . . everything about you."

The ache within her burned, but before she could respond, his palms, still pressed against her cheeks, tilted her face upward. Slowly, he touched her lips with his. Warm and pliant, they promised a future together—she could feel it!

Shawna's heart began to race.

His lips moved slowly and cautiously at first, as if he were exploring and discovering her for the first time.

Tears welled unbidden to her eyes and she moaned, leaning closer to him, feeling her breath hot and constricted in her lungs.

Love me, she cried mutely. *Love me as you did.*

The kiss was so innocent, so full of wondering, she felt as flustered and confused as a schoolgirl. "I love you," she whispered, her fingers gripping his shoulders as she clung to him and felt hot tears slide down her cheeks. "Oh, Parker, I love you!"

His arms surrounded her, drawing her downward until she was half lying across him, listening to the beat of his heart and feeling the hard muscles of his chest.

The sheets wrinkled between them as Parker's lips sought hers, anxious and moist, pressing first against her mouth and then lower, to the length of her throat as his hands twined in the golden sun-bleached strands of her hair. "I have the feeling I don't deserve you," he murmured into her ear, desire flaring in his brilliant blue eyes.

From the hallway, Jake cleared his throat. Shawna glanced up to see her brother, shifting restlessly from one foot to the other as he stood just outside the door.

"I, uh, hope I'm not disturbing anything," he said, grinning from one ear to the other, his hands stuffed into the pockets of his cords as he sauntered into the small room.

Shawna hurriedly wiped her cheeks. "Your timing leaves a lot to be desired."

"So I've been told," he replied, before glancing at Parker. "So, how's the patient?"

"Grumpy," Shawna pronounced.

"He didn't look too grumpy to me." Jake snatched a shiny red apple from a fruit basket and polished it against his tweed sports jacket.

"You didn't see him barking at the orderly."

One side of Jake's mouth curved cynically as he glanced at Parker. "Not you, not the 'ice man.' " Still grinning, he bit into the apple.

"This place doesn't exactly bring out the best in me," Parker said, eyeing the man who had almost become his brother-in-law.

"Obviously," Shawna replied. "But if everything goes well in physical therapy today and tomorrow, and you don't get on Dr. Handleman's bad side again, you'll be out of here by the end of the week, only doing physical therapy on an outpatient basis."

"No wonder he's in a bad mood," Jake said, taking another huge bite from the apple. "Outpatient physical therapy sounds as bad as the seventh level of hell, if you ask me."

"No one did," Shawna reminded him, but smiled at her brother anyway. Jake had a way of helping her find humor in even the most trying times. Even as children, she could count on him and his cock-eyed sense of humor to lift her spirits even on her worst days.

Jake tossed his apple core deftly into a trash can. "Two points—or was that three?" he asked. When neither Parker nor Shawna answered, he shoved his fingers through his hair. "Boy, you guys are sure a cheery group."

"Sorry," Shawna said. "As I told you, Grumpy isn't in a great mood."

Jake glanced from Shawna to Parker. "So, what can we do to get you back on your feet?"

"You're the psychiatrist," Parker replied stonily. "You tell me."

Shawna reached into her purse. "Maybe I can help." Ignoring her brother's questioning gaze, she reached into her purse and withdrew a thick packet of photographs. "I thought these might do the trick."

Her hands were shaking as one by one, she handed him the snapshots of the fair. Her heart stuck in her throat as she saw the pictures of herself, her long blond hair caught in the breeze, her green eyes filled with mischief as she clung to the neck of that white wooden stallion on the carousel and stretched forward, reaching and missing the brass ring with the fluttering ribbons.

Other photos, of Parker trying to catch a peanut in his mouth, of Parker flaunting his prized brass ring, and of the dark-eyed fortune-teller, beckoning them inside her ragtag tent, brought back her memories of the fair. Now, in the hospital room, only a little over two weeks later, the old-time fair seemed ages past, and the fortune-teller's prediction loomed over Shawna like a black cloak.

Parker studied each picture, his eyes narrowed on the images in the still shots. His brow furrowed in concentration.

Shawna held her breath. Couldn't he see the adoration shining in her eyes as she gazed into the camera? Or the loving way he had captured her on film? And what about the pictures of him, grinning and carefree? Wasn't it obvious that they had been two people hopelessly head over heels in love?

For a minute, she thought he reacted, that there

was a flicker of recognition in his gaze, but as suddenly as it had appeared, it was gone.

"Nothing?" she asked, bracing herself.

He closed his eyes. "No—not nothing," he said, his voice dry and distant. "But what we shared—what was there at the fair—it's . . . gone."

"Just misplaced," Jake said quickly as if feeling the searing wound deep in Shawna's soul. "You'll find it again."

"I'd like to think so," Parker admitted, but he still seemed vexed, his thick brows knitted, his chin set to one side, as if he were searching for a black hole in the tapestry her pictures had woven.

"Look, I've got to run," Jake said quickly, looking at his sister meaningfully. "Mom and Dad are expecting you for dinner tonight."

"But I can't," she said, unable to leave Parker. She felt that if she were given just a few more minutes, she could cause the breakthrough in Parker's memory.

"Don't stay on my account," Parker cut in, glaring angrily at the pictures spread across his bed.

Shawna saw them then as he did, pictures of a young couple in love, their future bright and untarnished, and she cringed inside, knowing instinctively what he felt—the anger and the resentment, the pain and the blackness of a time he couldn't remember.

"Maybe I shouldn't have brought these," she said hurriedly, scooping the photographs into the purse.

He snatched one out of her hands, the photo of her with her face flushed, her long hair billowing over the neck of the glossy white carousel horse. "I'll keep this one," he said, his features softening a little, "if you don't mind."

"You're sure?"

"Positive."

"Let's go." Jake suggested. "You can come back later. But right now, Mom and Dad are waiting."

Shawna felt her brother's hand over her arm, but she twisted her neck, craning to stare at Parker who didn't move, just studied the photograph in his hands. Impatiently, Jake half dragged her through the building.

"That was a stupid move!" Jake nearly shouted, once they were outside the hospital. "He's not ready for pictures of the past, can't you see that?" Jake's expression turned dark as he opened the car door for her, then slid behind the wheel and shoved the Porsche into gear.

"You can't just skip into his room and hand him pictures of a rose-colored future that could have been, you know. It takes time! Think about him, not just yourself! Where's your professionalism, *Doctor*?"

"Back in my medical bag, I guess," Shawna said, staring blindly out the windows. "I'm sorry."

"It's not me you have to apologize to." He let out a long, disgusted breath, then patted her shoulder. "Just hang in there. Try to think of Parker as another patient—not your fiancé, okay?"

"I will, but it's hard."

"I know," he said, "but he needs all your strength now—and your patience." Jake turned off the main highway and veered down the elm-lined driveway of his parents' house. "Okay, Sis. Show's on. Stiff upper lip for Mom and Dad," he teased, reaching across her and pushing open the car door.

As Shawna walked up the flagstone path, she steadfastly shoved all her doubts aside. Tomorrow she'd see Parker again and when she did, she wouldn't push too hard. She'd be patient and wait until the walls blocking his memory eroded—even if it killed her.

Long after Shawna left his room, Parker stared at the small photograph in his hand. Without a doubt, Dr. Shawna McGuire was the most fascinating, beautiful, and stubborn woman he'd ever met.

He knew now why he'd fallen in love with her. Though he was loath to admit it and despite all the problems he now faced, he was falling in love with her again. The depth of his feelings was a surprise. She aroused him sensually as well as intellectually. Doctor McGuire, though she professed her love, was a challenge. Just being near her, smelling her perfume, seeing the glimmer of mystique in her intelligent green eyes, was enough to drive him to distraction and cause an uncomfortable heat to rise in his loins.

Unfortunately, he had to be careful. No longer was he a recent tennis star with a future bright as the sun, acting in commercials and coaching younger, up-coming athletes. Now his future was unsure.

He glanced down and the woman in the photograph smiled up at him. She swore she loved him and he believed her. And, if he let himself, he could easily get caught in her infectious enthusiasm. Several times, when he'd kissed her, he'd seen images in his mind—smelled the salty air of the beach, or fresh raindrops in her hair, heard the tinkle of her laughter, felt the driving beat of her heart. Reality mixed with sights and smells that were as elusive as a winking star—bright one minute, dim and clouded the next.

And now, lying in the hospital bed, with months, perhaps years of physical therapy staring him in the face, what could he offer her?

A big fat nothing. Because no matter how she deluded herself, Shawna was wrong about one thing: Parker would never be the man he was before the accident. His perception, with his memory, had changed.

Brad Lomax was gone, as was Parker's ability to coach and play tennis. The man Shawna McGuire had fallen in love with no longer existed and this new man—the one who couldn't even remember her— was a pale substitute. How long could she love a faded memory, he wondered. When would that love, so freely given, turn to duty?

Glancing again at the woman in the picture, Parker ached inside. Yes, he wanted her, maybe even loved her. But he wouldn't let her live a lie, sacrifice herself because she believed in a dream that didn't exist.

Gritting his teeth, Parker took the snapshot of Shawna and crushed it in his fist—then feeling immediately contrite, he tried to press the wrinkles from the photo and laid it, face down, in a book someone had left by his bed.

"Help me," he prayed, his voice echoing in the empty room. "Help me be whole again."

Six

Shawna snatched a patient's chart from the rack next to the door of the examination room. She was running late and had to force herself into gear. "Get a move on, doctor," she muttered under her breath as she glanced quickly over the patient information file. The patient, Melinda James, was new to the clinic, had an excellent health record, and was eighteen years old.

"Good afternoon," Shawna said, shoving open the door to find a beautiful black-haired girl with round eyes perched on the edge of the examination table. She looked scared as her fingers clamped nervously over a sheet she'd pulled over her shoulders, and Shawna felt as if the girl wanted to bolt. "I'm Dr. McGuire," she said calmly. "And you're Melinda?"

Melinda nodded and chewed nervously on her lip.

"So what can I do for you?"

"I, uh, saw your name in the paper," Melinda said quickly, glancing away. "You're the doctor who's engaged to Parker Harrison, right?"

Shawna's stomach tightened at the mention of Parker. Was Melinda a reporter, pretending to be a patient just to get an inside story on Parker, or was there something else?

"That's right, but I really don't see what that has to do with anything." She clamped the chart to her chest. "Do you know Parker?"

"He's got amnesia, doesn't he?"

Shawna tried to keep her tongue in check. Obviously the girl was nervous—maybe she was just making conversation. "I can't discuss Parker's condition. Now—" she glanced down at her chart. "Is there a reason you came to see me? A health reason?"

The girl sighed. "Yes I, uh, I've only been in Portland a few months so I don't have a doctor here. I went to a pediatrician in Cleveland," Melinda continued, "but I'm too old for a pediatrician now and I've got this problem, so I made an appointment with you."

"Fair enough." Shawna relaxed a little and took a pen from the pocket of her lab coat. "What was the pediatrician's name?"

Melinda seemed hesitant.

"I'll need this information in case we need to contact him for his files," Shawna explained, offering the girl an encouraging smile.

"Rankin, Harold Rankin," Melinda said quickly and Shawna scrawled the physician's name in the appropriate spot on the form. "Thanks." Pushing her suspicions aside, Shawna set the chart on a cabinet. "You said you had a problem. What kind of problem?"

Melinda twisted the sheet between her fingers. "I'm sick." Avoiding Shawna's eyes, she said in a rush, "I can't keep anything down and I'm not anoretic or whatever it's called. I don't understand what's wrong. I've had the flu for over a month and it just won't go away. I've never been sick for this long."

"The flu?" Shawna said, eyeing the girl's healthy skin color and clear eyes. "You're feverish? Your muscles ache?"

"No, not really. It's just that one minute I'm feeling great; the next I think I might throw up."

"And do you?"

"Sometimes—especially in the afternoon." Melinda wrung her hands anxiously together and sweat beaded her forehead. "And sometimes I get horrible cramps."

"Anything else? Sore throat?"

Shaking her short glossy hair, Melinda sighed. "I kept hoping I would get better, but—" She shrugged and the sheet almost slipped from her fingers.

"Well, let me take a look at you. Lie down."

Shawna spent the next fifteen minutes examining Melinda carefully, as the girl nearly jumped off the examination table each time she was touched.

"When was the date of your last menstrual period?" Shawna finally asked, once the examination was over and Melinda was sitting, sheet draped over her on the table.

"I don't know. A couple of months ago, I guess."

"You *guess*?" Shawna repeated.

"I don't keep track—I'm real irregular."

"How irregular?"

"Well, not every month. A skip around a little."

"Could you be pregnant?"

Melinda's eyes widened and she licked her lips. "I—I don't get sick in the morning. Never in the morning."

Shawna smiled, trying to put the girl at ease. "It's different with everyone. I had a patient who only was sick at night."

Melinda chewed on her lower lip. "I—uh, it's possible, I guess," she whispered.

"Why don't we run a quick test and see?" Shawna asked.

"When will I know?"

"In a little while. I have a friend in the lab. The pregnancy test is relatively easy; but if there's something else, we won't know about it for a couple of days. Now, why don't you try to remember the date of your last period."

Melinda closed her eyes as Shawna drew a small vial of blood from her arm and had a nurse take the filled vial to the lab.

"I don't know. I think it was around the Fourth of July."

Shawna wasn't surprised. All of Melinda's symptoms pointed toward pregnancy. "This is nearly October," she pointed out.

Melinda's lower lip protruded defiantly. "I said I was irregular."

"Okay. No need to worry about it, until we know for sure." She checked her watch. "It's still early— the hospital lab can rush the results if I ask."

"Would you?"

"Sure. You can get dressed and meet me in my office in a few hours—say four o'clock?"

"Fine." Melinda grudgingly reached for her clothes and Shawna, feeling uneasy, left the room.

By the time Shawna returned to her office after seeing the rest of her patients and finished some paperwork, she was ready to call it a day. It was four o'clock and she was anxious to drive to Mercy Hospital to spend some time with Parker.

But first she had to deal with Melinda James.

"Well?" Melinda asked as she plopped into the chair opposite Shawna's desk.

Shawna scanned the report from the lab, then glanced at the anxious girl.

"Your test was positive, Melinda. You're going to have a baby."

Melinda let out a long sigh and ran her fingers through her hair. "I can't believe it," she whispered, but her voice lacked conviction and for the first time Shawna wondered if Melinda had been suspicious of her condition all along. "There's no chance that" —she pointed to the pink report—"is wrong."

"Afraid not."

"Great," Melinda mumbled, blinking back tears.

"I take it this isn't good news."

"The worst! My dad'll kill me!"

"Maybe you're underestimating your dad," Shawna suggested.

"No way!"

"What about the father of your child?" Shawna asked.

Tears flooded the girl's eyes. "The father?" she repeated, swallowing with difficulty and shaking her head.

"He has the right to know."

"He can't," Melinda said, her voice low and final, as if she had no choice in the matter.

"Give him a chance."

Melinda's eyes were bright with tears. "I can't tell him," she said. "He thinks this is all my responsibility. The last thing he wants is a baby."

"You don't know—"

"Oh, yes I do. He said so over and over again."

Shawna handed her a couple of tissues and Melinda dabbed her eyes but was unable to stem the flow of her tears.

"I—I was careful," she said, blinking rapidly. "But he'll blame me, I know he will!"

"Sometimes a man changes his mind when he's actually faced with the news that he's going to be a father."

"But he can't!" Melinda said harshly, obviously hurting deep inside.

Shawna walked around the desk and placed her arm around the young woman's shaking shoulders. "I don't want to pry," she said evenly. "What's going on between you and the father isn't any of my business—"

"If you only knew," Melinda whispered, glancing at Shawna with red-rimmed eyes, then shifting her gaze. Standing, she pushed away Shawna's arm. "This is my problem," she said succinctly. "I—I'll handle it."

"Try not to think of the baby as a problem, okay?" Shawna advised, reaching for a card from a small holder on her desk. "Take this card—it has Dr. Chambers's number. He's one of the best obstetricians in the city."

"What I need now is a shrink," Melinda said, still sniffing.

"My brother's a psychiatrist," Shawna said quietly, locating one of Jake's business cards. "Maybe you should talk with him—"

Melinda snatched the cards from Shawna's outstretched hand. "I—I'll think about it. After I talk with the father."

Shawna offered the girl an encouraging smile. "That's the first step."

"Just remember—this was *your* idea!"

"I'll take full responsibility," Shawna replied, but read the message in the young woman's eyes. More clearly than words, Melinda had told her Shawna didn't know what she was saying. Anger and defiance bright in her eyes, Melinda James walked briskly out the door.

Shawna watched her leave and felt the same nagging doubts she had when she'd first talked to the girl. "You can't win 'em all," she told herself thoughtfully as she hung her lab coat in the closet and quickly ran a brush through her hair. But she couldn't shake the feeling that Melinda, despite her vocal doubts, had known she was pregnant all along.

She reached for her purse and slung it over her shoulder, but stopped before slipping her arms through her jacket. Feeling a little guilty, she called directory assistance in Cleveland and asked for the number of Harold Rankin, Melinda's pediatrician.

"There are several H. Rankins listed," the operator told her.

"I'm looking for the pediatrician. He must have an office number."

The operator paused. "I'm sorry. There is no Doctor Rankin listed in Cleveland."

"Unlisted? Look, I'm a doctor myself. I need to consult with him about a patient and I don't have his number," Shawna said, new suspicions gnawing at her.

The operator muttered something under her breath. "I really can't—"

"It's important!"

"Well, I guess I can tell you this much, there's no Dr. Harold Rankin listed or unlisted in Cleveland. Just a minute." For a few seconds all Shawna could hear was clicking noises. "I'm sorry—I checked the suburbs. No Dr. Harold Rankin."

"Thank you," Shawna whispered, replacing the receiver. So Melinda had lied—or the doctor had moved. But that was unlikely. Shawna remembered Melinda's first words. *"I saw your name in the paper. . . . You're the doctor who's engaged to Parker Harrison, aren't you? . . . He's got amnesia, right?"*

Without thinking about what she was doing, Shawna buttoned her jacket and half ran out the door of her office. She waved good-bye to the receptionist, but her mind was filled with Melinda's conversation and the girl's dark grudging glances. No, Melinda James wasn't a reporter, but she was hiding something. Shawna just couldn't figure out what it was.

As she took the elevator down to the underground parking garage, she was alone, her keys gripped in one hand. What did a pregnant eighteen-year-old girl have to do with Parker? she asked herself, suddenly certain she wouldn't like the answer.

Parker's leg throbbed, rebelling against his weight as he attempted to walk the length of the physical therapy room. His hands slipped on the cold metal bars, but he kept himself upright, moving forward by sheer will. Every rigid, sweat-covered muscle in his body screamed with the strain of dragging his damned leg, but he kept working.

"That's it, just two more steps," a pert therapist with a cheery smile and upturned nose persuaded, trying to encourage him forward.

Gritting his teeth he tried again, the foot slowly lifting from the floor. Pain ripped through his knee and he bit his lower lip, tasting the salt of his sweat. *Come on, Harrison,* he said to himself, squeezing his eyes shut, *do it for Shawna, that beautiful lady doctor who's crazy enough to love you.*

In the past few weeks, he'd experienced flashes of memory, little teasing bits which had burned in his mind. He could remember being with her on a sailboat—her tanned body, taut and sleek. She'd been leaning against the boom as the boat skimmed across clear green water. Her blond hair had billowed around her head, shimmering gold in the late afternoon sun, and she'd laughed, a clear sound that rippled across the river.

Even now, as he struggled to the end of the parallel bars, he could remember the smell of fresh water and perfume, the taste of her skin and the feel of her body, warm and damp, as she'd lain with him on the sand of some secluded island.

Had they made love? That one delicious recollection escaped him, rising to the surface only to sink below the murky depths of his memory, as did so much of his life. Though he knew—he could sense—that he'd loved her, there was something else stopping him from believing everything she told him of their life together—something ugly and unnamed and a part of the Brad Lomax tragedy.

"Hey! You've done it!" the therapist cried as Parker took a final agonizing step.

While thinking of the enigma that was his relationship with Shawna, he hadn't realized that he'd finished his assigned task. "I'll be damned," he muttered.

"You know what this means, don't you?" the therapist asked, positioning a wheelchair near one of the contraptions that Parker decided were designed for the sole purpose of human torture.

"What?"

"You're a free man. This is the final test. Now, if your doctor agrees, you can go home and just come back here for our workouts."

Parker wiped the sweat from his eyes and grinned. He'd be glad to leave this place! Maybe once he was home he'd start to remember and he could pick up the pieces of his life with Shawna. Maybe then the dreams of a mystery woman that woke him each night would disappear, and the unknown past would become crystal clear again.

The therapist tossed him a white terry towel and a nurse appeared.

Parker wiped his face, then slung the towel around his neck.

Placing her hands on the handles of the wheelchair, the nurse said, "I'll just push you back to your room—"

"I'll handle that," Shawna said. She'd been standing in the doorway, one shoulder propped against the jamb as she watched Parker will himself through the therapy. She'd witnessed the rigid strength of his sweat-dampened shoulders and arms, seen the flinch of pain as he tried to walk, and recognized the glint of determination in his eyes as he inched those final steps to the end of the bars.

"If you're sure, Doctor—" the nurse responded, noting Shawna's identification tag.

"Very sure." Then she leaned over Parker's shoulder and whispered, "Your place or mine?"

He laughed then. Despite the throb of pain in his

knee and his anguish of not being able to remember anything of his past, he laughed. "Get me out of here."

"Your wish is my command." Without further prompting, she rolled him across the polished floors of the basement hallway and into the waiting elevator, where the doors whispered closed. "Alone at last," she murmured.

"What did I do to deserve you?" he asked, glancing up at her, his eyes warm and vibrant.

Her heart constricted and impulsively she jabbed the stop button before leaning over and pressing her lips to his. "You have been, without a doubt, the best thing that ever happened to me," she said, swallowing back a thick lump in her throat. "You showed me there was more to life than medical files, patient charts, and trying to solve everyone else's problems."

"I can't believe—"

"Of course not," she said, laughing and guessing that he was going to argue with her again, tell her he didn't deserve her love. "You've been right all along, Parker," she confided. "Everything I've been telling you is a lie. You don't deserve me at all. It's just that I'm a weak, simple female and you're so strong and sexy and macho!"

"Is that so?" he asked, strong arms dragging her into his lap.

She kissed him again, lightly this time. "Well, isn't that what you wanted to hear?"

"Sounded good," he admitted.

Cocking her head to one side, her blond hair falling across his shoulder, she grinned slowly. "Well, the strong and sexy part is true."

"But somehow I don't quite see you as a 'weak, simple female.'"

"Thank heaven. So just believe that you're the best thing in my life, okay? And no matter what happens, I'm never going to take the chance of losing you again!"

"You won't," he murmured, pulling her closer, claiming her lips with a kiss so intense her head began to spin. She forgot the past and the future. She could only concentrate on the here and now, knowing in her heart the one glorious fact that Parker, her beloved Parker, was holding her and kissing her as hungrily as he had before the accident—as if he did indeed love her all over again.

Her breath caught deep in her lungs and inside, she was warming, feeling liquid emotion rush through her veins. She felt his hands move over her, rustling the lining of her skirt to splay against her back, hold her in that special, possessive manner that bound them so intimately together. Delicious, wanton sensations whispered through her body and she tangled her hands in his hair.

"Oh, what you do to me," he whispered in a voice raw and raspy as his fingers found the hem of her sweater and moved upward to caress one swollen breast. Hot and demanding, his fingers touched the soft flesh and Shawna moaned softly as ripples of pleasure ran like wildfire through her blood.

"Parker, please—" She cradled his head against her, feeling the warmth of his breath touch her skin. His lips teased one throbbing peak, his tongue moist as it caressed the hard little button.

Shawna was melting inside. Rational thought ceased and she was only aware of him and the need he created.

"Oh, Shawna," he groaned, slowly releasing her,

his eyes still glazed with passion as a painful memory sizzled through his desire. "You're doing it again," he whispered, rubbing his temple as if it throbbed. "Shawna—stop!"

She had trouble finding her breath. Her senses were still spinning out of control and she stung from his rejection. Why was he pulling away from her? "What are you talking about?"

Passion-drugged eyes drilled into hers. "I remember, Shawna."

Relieved, she smiled. Everything was going to be fine. She tried to stroke his cheek but he jerked away. "Then you know how much we loved each—"

"I remember that you teased me, pushed me to the limit in public places. Like this."

"Parker, what are you talking about?" she cried, devastated. What was he saying? If he remembered, then surely he'd know how much she cared.

"It's not all clear," he admitted, helping her to her feet. "But there were times, just like this, when you drove me out of my mind!" He reached up and slapped the control panel. The elevator started with a lurch and Shawna nearly lost her footing.

"I don't understand—" she whispered.

The muscles of his face tautened. "Remember the fair?" he said flatly. "At the fir tree?"

She gasped, recalling rough bark against her bare back, his hands holding her wrists, their conversation about his "mistress."

"It was only a game we played," she said weakly.

"Some game." His eyes, still smoldering with the embers of recent passion, avoided hers. "You know, somehow I had the impression that you and I loved each other before—that we were lovers. You let me think that." His eyes were as cold as the sea.

"We were," she said, then recognized the censure in the set of his jaw. "Well, almost. We'd decided to wait to get married before going to bed."

Arching a brow disdainfully, he said through clenched teeth, "*We* decided? You're a doctor. I'm a tennis pro. Neither one of us is a kid and you expect me to believe that we were playing the cat-and-mouse game of waiting 'til the wedding."

"You said you remembered," she whispered, but then realized his memory was fuzzy. Certain aspects of their relationship were still blurred.

"I said I remembered part of it." But the anger in his words sounded hollow and unsure, as if he were trying to find an excuse to deny the passion between them only moments before.

The elevator car jerked to a stop and the doors opened on the fourth floor. Shawna, her breasts still aching, reached for the handles of the wheelchair, but Parker didn't wait for her. He was already pushing himself down the corridor.

In the room, she watched him shove the wheelchair angrily aside and flop onto the bed, his face white from the effort.

"You're memory is selective," she said, leaning over the bed, pushing her face so close to his that she could read the seductive glint in his blue eyes.

"Maybe," he admitted and stared at her lips, swallowing with difficulty.

"Then why won't you just try to give us a chance? We were good together, sex or no sex. Believe me." She heard him groan.

"Don't do this to me," he asked, the fire in his eyes rekindling.

"I'll do whatever I have to," she whispered, leaning

closer, kissing him, brushing the tips of her breasts across his chest until he couldn't resist.

"You're making a big mistake." He pressed her close to him.

"Let me."

"I'm not the same man—"

"I don't care, damn it," she said, then sighed. "Just love me."

"That would be too easy," he admitted gruffly, then buried his face in her hair, drinking in the sweet feminine smell that teased at his mind every night. He held her so fiercely she could feel the heat of his body through her clothes. Clinging to him, she barely heard the shuffle of feet in the doorway until Parker dragged his lips from hers and stared over her shoulder.

Twisting, half expecting to find Jake with his lousy sense of timing, she saw a young black-haired girl standing nervously on one foot, then the other.

"Melinda?" Shawna asked, her throat dry. "Are you looking for me?"

"No," Melinda James said quietly, her large, brown eyes lifting until they clashed with Parker's. "I came to see him, on your advice."

"My advice—what—?" But a dark doubt steadily grew in her heart and she gripped Parker's shoulders more tightly, as if by clinging to him, she could stop what was to come. "No—there must be some mistake," she heard herself saying, her voice distant, as if in a dream.

"You told me to talk to him and that's . . . that's why I'm here," Melinda said, her eyes round with fear, large tears collecting on her lashes. "You see, Parker Harrison is the father of my child."

Seven

"He's what?" Shawna whispered, disbelieving.

"It's true."

"Wait a minute—" Parker stared at the girl, not one flicker of recognition in his eyes. "Who are you?"

Shawna wanted to tell him not to believe a word of Melinda's story, but she didn't. Instead she forced herself to watch his reaction as Melinda, hesitantly at first, then with more conviction, claimed she and Parker had been seeing each other for several months, long before he'd started dating Shawna, and that she'd become pregnant with his child.

Parker blanched, his mouth drawing into a tight line.

"This is absurd," Shawna finally said, praying that Parker would back her up.

"How old are you?" he asked, eyes studying the dark-haired girl.

"Eighteen."

"Eighteen?" he repeated, stunned. His eyes narrowed and he forced himself to stand. "And you're saying that you and I—"

"—were lovers," Melinda clarified.

Shawna couldn't stand it a minute more. "This is all a lie. Parker, this girl came into my office, asked all sort of questions about you and your amnesia, and then had me examine her."

"And?"

"And she *is* pregnant. That much is true. But . . . but . . . she's lying . . . you couldn't have been with her. *I* would have known." But even though her words rang with faith, she couldn't help remembering all the times Parker had taunted her by pretending to have a mistress. *I suppose I'll have to give up my mistress*, he'd said at the fair, teasing her, but wounding her just the same. Her old doubts twisted her heart. Was it possible that he'd actually been seeing someone and that the person he'd been with had been this girl?

"You don't remember me?" Melinda asked.

Parker closed his eyes, flinching a bit.

"I saw you the night of the accident," she prodded. "You . . . you were with Brad and he was drunk."

Parker's eyes flew open and pain, deep and tragic, showed in their vibrant blue depths.

"You stopped by my apartment and Brad became violent, so you hauled him back to the car."

"She's making this up," Shawna said. "She must have read about it in the papers or heard it on the news." But her voice faltered as she saw Parker wrestling with a memory.

"I've met her before," he said slowly. "I was at her apartment."

"No!" Shawna cried. She wouldn't believe a word

of Melinda's lies—she couldn't! Parker would never betray her! She'd almost lost Parker once and she wasn't about to lose him again, not to this girl, not to anyone. "Parker, you don't honestly believe—"

"I don't know *what* to believe!" he snapped.

"But we've been through so much together . . ." Then she turned her eyes on Melinda and all of her professionalism and medical training flew out the window. No longer was Melinda her patient, but just a brash young woman trying to tarnish the one man Shawna loved. "Look," she said, her voice as ragged as her emotions. "I don't really know who you are or why you're here torturing him or even how you got into this room, but I want you out, now!"

"Stop it, Shawna," Parker said.

But Shawna ignored him. "I'll call the guards if I have to, but you have no right to come in here and upset any of the patients—"

"I'm *your* patient," Melinda said, satisfaction briefly gleaming in her eyes.

"I referred you to—"

"He's the father of my child, dammit!" Melinda cried, wilting against the wall and sobbing like the girl she was.

"She can stay," Parker pronounced as Tom Handleman, his lab coat flapping behind him, marched into the room. "What the devil's going on here?" he demanded, eyeing Shawna. "Who's she?" He pointed an accusing finger at the huddled figure of Melinda.

"A friend of mine," Parker said, his voice ringing with quiet authority.

"Parker, no!" Shawna whispered, ignoring Tom. "She lied to me this morning—told me the name of her previous physician in Cleveland. I tried to call him—there is no Dr. Harold Rankin in the area."

"Then he moved," Melinda said, stronger because of Parker's defense. "It's—it's been years."

"She has to leave," Shawna decided, turning to Tom, desperation contorting her face.

"Maybe she can help," Tom suggested.

"Help?" Shawna murmured. "She's in here accusing him, lying to him, lying to me—"

Melinda stood, squaring her shoulders and meeting Parker's clouded gaze. "I—I understand why you feel betrayed, Dr. McGuire. First Parker lied to you and then I had to lie this morning. But I just wanted to find out that he was all right. No one would let me in here. Then *you* convinced me that I had to tell him about the baby—"

"*Baby?*" Handleman asked, his face ashen.

"—and I decided you were right. Every father has the right to know about his child whether he wants to claim him or not."

"For cryin' out loud!" Tom whispered. "Look, Miss—"

"James," Melinda supplied.

"Let her stay," Parker said.

"You remember me," she said.

Shawna wanted to die as they stared at each other.

"I've met you," Parker admitted, his face muscles taut. "And I don't mean to insult you, Miss James—"

"Melinda. You called me Linnie. Don't you remember?" Her chin trembled and she fought against tears that slid from her eyes.

"I'm sorry—"

"You have to remember!" she cried. "All those nights by the river—all those promises—"

Good Lord, what was she saying? Shawna's throat closed up. "Parker and I were—are—going to be married, and neither one of us believes that he's the father of your child. This is obviously just some way for you and your boy friend to take advantage—"

"No!" Melinda whispered. "I don't care what *you* believe, but Parker loves me! He—he—" her eyes darted quickly around the room and she blinked. "Oh, please, Parker. Remember," she begged.

Parker gripped the arms of his wheelchair. "Melinda," he said softly. Was it Shawna's imagination or did his voice caress the younger woman's name? "I don't remember ever sleeping with you."

"You deny the baby?"

He glanced at Shawna, his eyes seeming haunted. She could only stare back at him. "Not the baby. I'm just not sure it's mine."

Shawna shook her head. "No—"

"Then maybe you'd want a simple paternity test," Melinda suggested.

"Hey—hold the phone," Tom Handleman cut in. "Let's all just calm down. Right now, Miss James, I'm asking you to leave." Then he glanced at Shawna. "You, too, Dr. McGuire. This has been a strain on Parker. Let's all just give it a rest."

"I'm afraid I can't do that," Melinda said staunchly, seeming to draw from an inner reserve of strength. "Don't get me wrong, Parker. I'm not interested in ruining your reputation or trying to damage your professional image, but my baby needs his father."

"So you want money," Parker said cynically.

"Money isn't what I'm after," Melinda said, and Shawna felt a chill as cold as a December wind cut through her. "I want to give my baby a name and I want him to know who his father is. If it takes a paternity test to convince you or a lawsuit, I don't care." Swallowing back a fresh onslaught of tears, she walked unsteadily out of the room.

Shawna turned a tortured gaze to Parker. "You remember her?"

He nodded and let his forehead drop to his hand. "A little."

Dying inside, Shawna leaned against the bed. After all these weeks, Parker still barely admitted to remembering *her*—only disjointed pieces of their relationship. And yet within fifteen minutes of meeting Melinda James he conceded that he recognized her. Dread settled over her.

Sick inside, she wondered if Melinda's ridiculous accusations could possibly be true. Did Parker remember Melinda because they had slept together? Was her face so indelibly etched in his mind because of their intimacy? But that was ridiculous—she knew it and deep down, so did he!

She felt that everything she'd believed in was slowly being shredded into tiny pieces.

"You—you and Brad. You saw her that night?" she asked, her voice barely audible over the sounds of the hospital.

He nodded, his jaw extending. "Yes."

"And you remember?"

"Not everything."

"Maybe she was Brad's girl. Maybe the baby is his."

Parker's eyes narrowed. "Maybe. I don't know."

Tom placed his hand over Shawna's arm and guided her to the door. "Don't torture yourself," he said in a concerned whisper. "Go home, think things through. I guarantee you Parker will do the same. Then tomorrow, come back and take him home."

"Home?" she repeated dully.

"Yes, I'm releasing him tomorrow." He glanced over his shoulder to Parker. "That is, unless Miss James's visit sets him back."

"I hope not," Shawna said, staring at Parker with new eyes, trying to smile and failing miserably. "Look, I really need to talk to him. Just a few minutes, okay?"

"I guess it won't hurt," Tom decided, "but keep it short. He's had one helluva shock today."

"Haven't we all?" Shawna said as Tom closed the door behind him.

Parker didn't look at her. He scowled through the window to the gray day beyond.

Had he betrayed her? Shawna couldn't believe it. Melinda had to be lying. But why? And why had Parker gone to visit the young girl before taking Brad home? Was it to call off their affair? Or had he needed to see her just one more time before the wedding? Shawna's stomach churned at the thought of them lying together, kissing—

"So much for the knight in shining armor, huh?" he mocked.

"I don't believe a word of her lies. And I really don't think you do, either."

"That's the tricky part," he admitted, staring up at the ceiling. "I know I've seen her—been with her, but—"

"—But you don't remember." Tossing her hair over her shoulder, she leaned against the bed.

"She has no reason to lie."

"Neither do I, Parker. I don't know anything about that girl, but I know what we shared and we didn't cheat or lie or betray one another."

"You're sure of that?"

"Positive," she whispered, wishing that awful shadow of doubt would disappear from her mind. "I only wish I could prove it."

Parker watched her blink back tears, saw her fine jaw jut in determination, and loved her for all of her pride and faith in him. Her blond hair draped across her shoulder to curl at her breast, and her eyes, fierce with indignation and bright with unshed tears, were as green as a night-darkened forest. How he loved her. Even lying here, charged with fathering another woman's child, he loved Shawna McGuire. But not because of any memories that had surfaced in his mind. No, this love was new, borne from just being near her. Never had he met any woman so proud and free-spirited, so filled with giving and fighting for what she believed in. And what she believed in was him.

"Do you think you're the father of Melinda's baby?" she finally asked, so close he could touch her.

"I don't know."

She blanched, as if in severe pain. Without thinking he took her hand in his and pulled her gently forward, so that she was leaning over him.

"But I do know that if I ever did anything that would hurt you this much, I have to be the worst bastard that ever walked the earth."

She swallowed. "You . . . you wouldn't."

"I hope to God you're right." His throat felt dry, and though the last thing he intended to do was kiss her again, he couldn't stop himself. He held her close, tilting her chin up with one finger and molding his mouth possessively over hers. "I don't want to ever hurt you, Shawna," he rasped hoarsely. "Don't let me."

"You won't." She felt the promise of his tongue as it gently parted her lips, then heard the sound of voices in the hall. She couldn't think when he held her, and she needed time alone to recover from the shock of Melinda James's announcement. Besides, she'd promised Dr. Handleman she wouldn't upset Parker. "Look, I don't want to, but I've got to go. Doctor's orders."

"To hell with doctor's orders," he muttered, his arms flexing around her, thwarting her attempts at escape.

"Don't mess with the medical profession," she warned, but the lilt she tried for didn't materialize in her voice.

"Not the whole profession," he said slowly, "just one very beautiful lady doctor."

Oh, Parker! Her throat thickened. "Later," she promised, kissing him lightly on the tip of the nose and hearing him moan in response.

"You're doing it again," he whispered.

"What?"

"Driving me crazy." His gaze slid down her body and stupidly, like a schoolgirl, she blushed and ran for the door.

As she drove home, her thoughts were tangled in a web of doubt and despair. Was it possible? Could Melinda's story be true?

"Don't be absurd," she told herself as she maneuvered her little car through the twisted streets of Sellwood. Maple and alder trees had begun to drop their leaves, splashing the wet streets with clumps of gold, brown, and orange.

As Shawna climbed out of the car, a cold autumn breeze lifted her hair from her face, cooled the heat in her cheeks.

"Hey, about time you showed up!" Jake accosted her as he climbed out of a battered old Chevy pickup. "I thought you'd be home half an hour ago."

She'd forgotten all about him, and the fact that he'd offered to help her move. "I—I'm sorry. Uh, something came up," she said, trying to concentrate.

"Oh, yeah?" Jake's brows raised expectantly. "Don't tell me the coach is gonna be released."

"Tomorrow," Shawna said, her voice catching before her brother saw the pain in her eyes.

"Hey—whoa. What happened?" Jake grabbed both her shoulders, then forced her chin upward with one finger and stared down at her.

"You wouldn't believe it."

"Try me." One arm over her shoulders, Jake walked her to the front door and unlocked the dead bolt. The apartment was a mess. Boxes and bags were scattered all over the living-room floor, piled together with pictures, furniture, and clothes.

Shawna flopped in the nearest corner and told Jake everything, from the moment Melinda James had walked into her office until the time when she'd dropped the bomb about Parker being the father of her unborn child.

"And you bought that cockamamy story?"Jake asked, flabbergasted.

"Of course not." Shawna felt close to tears again.

"I hope not! It's ridiculous."

"But Parker did."

"*What?*"

"He claims to remember her, and admits that he visited her the night Brad was killed!"

Stricken, Jake sat on a rolled carpet. His eyes narrowed thoughtfully. "I don't believe it."

"Neither did I, but you should have been there."
Outside, Maestro meowed loudly. "I'm coming,"
Shawna called, every muscle in her body suddenly
slack as she tried to stand and couldn't.

"I'll let him in." Jake opened the door and the
bedraggled yellow tabby, wet from the rain, dashed
into the house and made a beeline for Shawna. He
cried until she petted him. "At least I can trust you,"
she said, her spirits lifting a little as the tabby washed
his face and started to purr noisily.

"You can trust Parker, too," Jake said. "You and I
both know it. That guy's crazy about you."

"Tell him," she said.

Jake frowned at his sister. "Okay, so this lunatic
girl has made some crazy claims and Parker can't
remember enough to know that she's lying. It's not
the end of the world." He caught her glance and
sighed. "Well, almost the end," he admitted, and
even Shawna had to smile. "Now, come on. What's
your next step?"

"You're not going to like it," Shawna said, opening a can of cat food for the cat.

"Try me."

"When the movers come tomorrow, I'm going to
have them take my things to Parker's."

"His house?" Jake asked, his brows shooting up.
"Does he know about this?"

"Nope." She straightened and her gaze narrowed
on her brother. "And don't you tell him about it."

"I wouldn't dare," Jake said with obvious respect
for Parker's volatile temper. "What about Mom and
Dad?"

"I'll explain."

"Good luck. That's one dogfight I don't want any
part of."

"I don't blame you." Why was this happening, and why now? She couldn't help thinking back to the Gypsy fortune-teller and her grim prediction.

"Shawna?" Jake asked, concern creasing his brow. "Are you okay?"

She nodded, her chin inching upward proudly. "I'm fine," she said. "I just have to stick by Parker 'til all of this is resolved one way or the other."

"Can I help?"

"Would you mind taking care of Maestro, just for a few days?"

Jake eyed the tabby dubiously. As if understanding he was the center of attention, Maestro leaped to the counter and arched his back as he rubbed up against the windowsill.

"I'm allergic to cats."

"He's outside most of the time."

"Bruno will eat him alive."

Shawna couldn't help but laugh. Bruno was a large mutt who was afraid of his own shadow. "Bruno will stick his big tail between his legs and run in the other direction."

"Okay."

"By the way," she said, feeling better. "You should work on that dog's obvious case of paranoia!"

"Maybe I should work on yours," Jake said, clapping her on the back. "You and I both know that Parker wasn't unfaithful to you."

"But he doesn't know it," Shawna replied, her convictions crumbling a little.

"You'll just have to convince him."

"I'm trying. Believe me." She pushed her hair from her eyes and rested the back of her head against the wall. "But that's not the only problem. What about

Melinda and her baby? Why is she lying? How does Parker know her? As much as this mess angers me, I can't forget that Melinda is only eighteen, unmarried, and pregnant."

"Does she have any family?"

"I don't know." Shawna blew a strand of hair from her eyes. "All she said was that her dad would kill her when he found out. I think she was just using a turn of phrase. At least I hope so."

"But you're not sure."

"That's one of the most frustrating things about all of this. I don't know a thing about her. I've never even heard her name before and now she claims to be carrying my fiancé's child."

"Maybe there's something I could do."

"Such as?"

"I don't know, but *something*."

"Not this time," she decided, grateful for his offer. "But thanks. This one I've got to handle by myself."

"I don't believe it!" Doris McGuire exclaimed. Sitting on her antique sofa, she stared across the room at her daughter. "Parker, and some, some girl?"

"That's what she claims," Shawna said.

"She's lying!"

"Who is?" Malcolm McGuire opened the front door and shook the rain from his hat, then tossed the worn fedora over the arm of an oak hall tree in the foyer. "Who's lying?" he repeated as he strode into the den and kissed Shawna's cheek. "You're not talking about Parker, are you?"

"Indirectly," Shawna admitted.

"Some young girl claims she's pregnant with Parker's child!" Doris said, her mouth pursed, her eyes bright with indignation. "Can you believe it?"

"Hey, slow down a minute," Malcolm said. "Let's start at the beginning."

As Shawna explained everything that had happened since she'd first met Melinda, Malcolm splashed a stiff shot of Scotch into a glass, thought twice about it, and poured two more drinks, which he handed to his daughter and wife.

"You don't believe it, do you?" he finally asked, searching Shawna's face.

"Of course not."

"But you've got doubts."

"Wouldn't you?"

"Never!" Doris declared. Malcolm's face whitened a bit.

"Sometimes a man can make a mistake, you know," he said.

"He was *engaged* to Shawna, for goodness sake!"

"But not married to her," Malcolm said slowly.

"Dad?" Did he know something? She studied the lines of her father's face as he finished his drink and sat heavily on the edge of the couch.

"I have no idea what Parker was up to," Malcolm said. "But I warned you that we didn't know all that much about him, didn't I? Maybe he had another girlfriend, I don't know. I would never have believed it before, but now? Why would she lie?"

Why indeed?

"But let's not judge him too harshly," Malcolm said. "Not until all the facts are in."

"I don't think you understand the gravity of the situation," Doris replied.

"Of course I do. Now, tell me about Parker. What does he have to say?"

"Not much." Shawna told her parents about the scene in the hospital room.

Malcolm cradled his empty glass in both hands and frowned into it. Doris shook her head and sighed loudly, though her back was ramrod stiff. "He'll just have to submit to a paternity test—prove the child isn't his and then get on with his life."

"Maybe it's not that simple," Malcolm said quietly. "He has a career to think of. All this adverse publicity might affect it."

"We're talking about the man Shawna plans to marry," Doris cut in, simmering with fury, "and here you are defending his actions—if, indeed, he was involved with that . . . that *woman*!"

"She's barely more than a girl," Shawna said.

"Eighteen is old enough to know better!"

Malcolm held up his hand to calm his wife. "I'm just saying we should all keep a level head."

Now that she'd said what she had to say, Shawna snatched her jacket from the back of a wing chair. "I think Dad's right—we should just low-key this for now."

"The girl is pregnant!"

"I know, I know. But I've decided that what I'm going to do is try and help Parker through this. It's got to be as hard on him as it is on me. That's one of the reasons I've decided to move in with him."

"Do what?" Doris was horrified. She nearly dropped her drink and her pretty face fell.

"He's being released from the hospital tomorrow. And I'm taking him home—to his house—with me."

"But you can't—you're not married. And now, with that girl's ridiculous accusations—"

"All the more reason to try and help jog his memory." Shawna saw the protests forming on her mother's lips and waved them off.

"Look, I've already made up my mind. If things had turned out differently, I'd already be married to him and living in that house. He and I would still have to deal with Melinda—unless this is all a convenient story of hers just because he's lost his memory. So, I'm going to stand by him. I just wanted you to know how to get in touch with me."

"But—"

"Mom, I love him." Shawna touched her mother's shoulder. It felt stiff and rigid under Doris's cotton sweater. "I'll call you in a couple of days."

Then, before her mother or father could try to change her mind, she walked out of the room, swept her purse off an end table, and opened the front door. She was glad to drive away from her parents' house because she needed time alone, time to think and clear her head. Tomorrow she'd have the battle of her life with Parker. He'd already told her he didn't want her tied to him as a cripple, that they couldn't marry until he was strong enough to support them both. Now, after Melinda's allegations, he'd be more adamant than ever.

Well, that was just too damned bad. Shawna intended to stand by him no matter what, and if he never walked again, she still intended to marry him. All she had to do was convince him that she was right. Involuntarily, she crossed her fingers.

Parker shoved the dinner tray aside. He wasn't hungry and didn't feel like trying to force food down his throat. With a groan, he reached for the crutches near his bed.

Dr. Handleman and the idiot down in physical therapy didn't think he was ready for crutches, but he'd begged them off a candy striper. Tomorrow he was going home and he wasn't about to be wheeled down the hall like a helpless invalid.

Gritting his teeth against a stab of pain in his knee, he slid off the bed and shoved the crutches under his arms. Then, slowly, he moved across the room, ignoring the throbbing in his knee and the erratic pounding of his heart. Finally he fell against the far wall, sweating but proud that he'd accomplished the small feat of walking across the room.

Breathing hard, he glanced out the window to the parking lot below. Security lamps glowed blue, reflecting on the puddles from a recent shower. Parker had a vague recollection of another storm. . . .

Rain had been drizzling down a windshield, wipers slapping the sheeting water aside as he had driven up a twisting mountain road. Someone—was it Brad?—had been slumped in the passenger seat. The passenger had fallen against Parker just as the Jeep had rounded a corner and there, right in the middle of the road, a huge truck with bright glaring headlights was barreling toward them, out of control. The truck driver blasted his horn, brakes squealed and locked, and Parker, reacting by instinct alone, had wrenched hard on the wheel, steering the Jeep out of the path of the oncoming truck and through the guardrail into the black void beyond.

Now, as he stood with his head pressed to the glass, Parker squeezed his eyes shut tight, trying to dredge up the memories, put the ill-fitting pieces of his past into some order.

He remembered Melinda—he'd seen her that night.

But she was just a girl. Surely he wouldn't have slept with her!

Impatient with his blank mind, he swore and knocked over one of his crutches. It fell against the table, knocking over a water glass and a book. From the pages of the book fluttered a picture—the single snapshot of Shawna on the carousel.

In the photograph, her cheeks were rosy and flushed, her eyes bright, her hair tossed wildly around her face. He'd been in love with her then. He could feel it, see it in her expression. And now, he'd fallen in love with her again and this time, he suspected, his feelings ran much deeper.

Despite the searing pain in his knee, he bent down, but the picture was just out of reach, in the thin layer of dust under the bed, and he couldn't coax the snapshot back to him, not even with the aid of his crutch.

He frowned at the irony. He couldn't reach the picture just as he couldn't have her, wouldn't chain her to a future so clouded and unsure. She deserved better than a man who might never walk without a cane—a man who couldn't even remember if he'd betrayed her.

Eight

Bracing herself, knowing full well that she was in for the fight of her life, Shawna walked into Parker's hospital room. "Ready?" she asked brightly.

"For what?" Parker was standing near his bed, fully dressed in gray cords and a cream-colored sweater, and balancing precariously on crutches.

"To go home." She picked up his duffel bag and tossed it over her shoulder, overlooking the storm gathering in his eyes. "Hurry up, I'm double-parked."

"I'll call a cab," he said quietly.

"No reason. Your house is on my way."

"To where?"

"The rest of my life."

Taking in a swift breath, he shoved one hand through his hair and shook his head. "You're unbelievable," he muttered.

"So you've said. Come on."

"Mr. Harrison?" A nurse pushed a wheelchair into his room and Parker swore under his breath.

America's most popular, most compelling romance novels...

Here, at last...love stories that really involve you!
Fresh, finely crafted novels with story lines so
believable you'll feel you're actually living them!
Characters you can relate to...exciting places to
visit...unexpected plot twists...all in all, exciting
romances that satisfy your mind and delight
your heart.

"I don't need *that*."

"Hospital regulations."

"Change them," he said, jaw tight.

"Come on, Parker, don't buck the system now," Shawna said, grabbing the handles of the wheelchair from the nurse. "Everyone has to use these chairs in order to get out."

Muttering to himself he slid into the chair and grumbled all the way along the corridor.

"I see we're in good spirits today," Shawna commented drily.

"Don't start in with that hospital 'we' talk, okay? I'm sick to death of it."

"My mistake. But don't worry. I'll probably make a few more before the day is over." She wheeled him into the elevator and didn't say a word until they were through the emergency room doors—the same door she'd run through weeks ago in her soggy wedding dress. That day felt like a lifetime ago.

Once they were in the car and through the parking lot, Shawna drove south, down the steep fir-cloaked hills of west Portland toward Lake Oswego and Parker's rambling Tudor house on the cliffs.

He stared out the window in silence, his eyes traveling over the familiar landscape. Leaves of the maple and oak trees had turned vibrant orange and brown, swirling in the wind and hanging tenaciously to black branches as Shawna drove toward the river. She glanced at Parker and noticed the tight pinch at the corners of his mouth and the lines of strain on his forehead as his stone house loomed into view.

Rising a full three stories, with a sharply gabled roof and dormers, the Tudor stood high on the cliffs overlooking the green waters of the Willamette. Trees and shrubbery flanked a broad, pillared porch and leaded glass windows winked in the pink rays from a setting sun.

Shawna cut the engine in front of the garage. She was reaching for the handle of her door when his voice stopped her.

"Aren't you going to ask me about Melinda?"

She froze and her stomach twisted painfully. Inadvertently she'd been avoiding the subject. "Is there something you want to tell me?"

Swallowing, he glanced away, then stared straight into her eyes. "I—I'm starting to remember," he admitted, weighing his words. "Part of the past is getting a little more clear."

She knew what was coming and died a bit inside, her fingers wrapping around the steering wheel as she leaned back in her seat. "The part with Melinda," she guessed, fingers clenched tight over the wheel.

"Yes."

"You . . . remember being with her?"

"Partly."

"Sleeping with her?"

She saw him hesitate, then shake his head. "No, but there's something . . . something about her. If only I could figure it out."

Licking her lips nervously, she forced her gaze to meet his. "I don't believe you betrayed me, Parker," she admitted, her voice rough. "I just can't."

"Maybe it would be easier if you did," he whispered.

"Why?"

"Because I feel—this tremendous responsibility."

She touched him then, her fingers light on his sweater, beneath which she could feel the coiled tension in his shoulders. "Give it time."

"I think we're running out." Then, as quickly as he'd brought up the subject, he jerked on the door handle and shoved the car door open. Cool wind invaded the interior as he gripped the frame and tried to struggle to his feet.

"Hey—wait!" She threw open her door and ran around the car just as he extracted himself from his seat and balanced on one leg, his face white with strain. "What do you think you're doing?" she demanded.

"Standing on my own," he said succinctly.

She caught his meaning, but refused to acknowledge it. "Sure, but you were almost flat on your face," she chastised. "How do you think Dr. Handleman would like it if you twisted that knee again and undid all his work?"

"I don't really give a damn what he does or doesn't like."

"Back to your charming sweet self, I see," she said, though her heart was pounding a rapid double-time. "Personally I'd hate to see you back in that hospital bed—in traction or worse—all because of your stupid, bullheaded male pride." She opened the hatchback of her car and wrestled with the collapsible wheelchair, noting that he'd paled slightly at the mention of the hospital. Good! He needed to think that one over. "So, quit being a child and enjoy being pampered."

"Pampered by whom?"

"Me." She locked the wheelchair and rolled it toward his side of the car.

"I don't want to be pampered."

"Oh, I think you will. Think of it as a reward for all those grueling hours you'll be spending with the physical therapist. I already hired him—he starts tomorrow."

"You did *what*?" Parker was livid, the fire in his eyes bright with rage. "I'm not going to—"

"Sure you are. And you're going to get off this self-reliant-male ego kick right now!"

She pushed the wheelchair next to him, but he held up a hand, spreading his fingers in her face. "Hold on, just one minute. I may not remember a lot about my past, but I know one thing, I never let any woman—even a lady doctor—push me around."

"Not even Melinda James?" Shawna snapped, instantly regretting her words when she saw his face slacken and guilt converge over his honed features.

"I'll deal with Melinda," he said, his voice ringing with authority, "in my own way." Then, ignoring the wheelchair, he reached down and tugged on the crutches she'd wedged into the car.

"You can't—"

"I can damned well do as I please, Dr. McGuire," he said cuttingly. "I'm not in a hospital any longer. You're not the boss." He slammed the crutches under his arms and swung forward, landing on his good leg with a jarring thud as he started up the flagstone path leading to the back door.

"You'll be back in the hospital before you know it if you don't watch out," she warned. Walking rapidly, she caught up with him.

"You can go home now, Shawna," he advised.

"I am."

Cocking his head to one side, he asked testily, "You're what?"

"Home."

"What?" he roared, twisting to look at her, his

crutch wedging in the chipped mortar to wrench out from under him. He pitched forward, grabbing frantically at the lowest branches of a nearby willow tree and landing with a thud on the wet grass.

"Parker!" Shawna knelt beside him. "I'm sorry—"

"Wasn't your fault." But he winced in pain, skin tight over his cheeks. "Now, tell me I heard wrong."

"I moved in this morning," she said, but her eyes were on his leg and without asking she pushed up his pant leg, to make sure that the stitches in his knee hadn't ruptured.

"I'm all right." He caught her wrist. "You are *not* my doctor. And you're not moving in here."

"Too late," she said, reaching into her pocket with her free hand and extracting a key ring from which dangled the keys to his house, car, and garage. "You gave these to me—for better or for worse, remember."

"We didn't get married."

"Doesn't matter. I'm committed to you, so you'd better get used to it!" She met his gaze steadily, her green eyes bright with defiance and pride. His fingers were still circling her wrist, warm against her skin, and her breathing, already labored, caught in her throat as his eyes moved from hers to the base of her neck and lower still. "Whether the ceremony happened or not, I consider myself your wife, and it will take an act of God for you to get rid of me."

"What about another woman's child?"

Her heart constricted. "We'll just have to deal with that together, won't we?" Nervously, she licked her lips, her self-confidence slowly drifting away.

He studied her mouth. "Maybe I need to stand alone before I can stand with someone," he said, sun glinting off the burnished strands of his hair.

"Are you telling me you won't let me live here?" She could barely concentrate. Her thoughts centered on her wrist and the provocative movement of his fingers against her skin. And his eyes, blue as the sea, stared into hers, smoldering with desire, yet bewildered.

"I just don't think we—you and I—can act like this accident didn't happen, pretending that Melinda James doesn't exist, that our lives will mesh in some sort of fairy-tale happy ending, when there are so many things pulling us apart." He glanced down at her lips and then to her hair, shining a radiant gold in the afternoon sunlight.

"Please, Parker, just give me a chance. I—I don't mean to come on like gangbusters, but we need time alone together, to work things out."

He pulled her close, kissing her as passionately as she'd ever been kissed, his lips possessive and strong with a fire she knew burned bright in his soul.

Responding, she cradled his head to hers, feeling the texture of his hair, and the warmth of his breath.

He shifted, more of his weight falling across her, his arms strong as they circled her waist.

"Parker, please—just love me," she whispered against his ear. He groaned a response. "Let me help you—help us." She placed both of her hands on his cheeks and held his head between her palms. "I can't let go, Melinda or no Melinda. Baby or no baby."

Before he could respond, Shawna heard the back door swing open and there, standing on the porch, her eyes dark with unspoken accusation, was Melinda James.

"What the devil?" Parker whispered. "How'd you—? Don't even answer! It doesn't matter."

Shawna realized that he'd probably given her a set of keys, too, long before he'd met Shawna, and the wound she'd tried so hard to bind opened again, fresh and raw.

"Remind me to have my locks changed," Parker muttered.

Shawna dusted off her skirt and tried to help him to his feet, but he pushed her hands aside, determined to stand by himself.

"I—I didn't know she would be here," Melinda said quietly, but her dark eyes darted quickly from Shawna to Parker and back again.

"I live here," Shawna said.

Melinda nearly dropped her purse. "You what?"

Parker's brows shot up. "Hold on a minute. I live here. Me. Alone."

"Not any more," Shawna said, cringing at how brash she sounded. Two months ago she would never have been so bold, but now, with her back against the wall and Parker's physical and mental health at stake, she'd fight tooth and nail to help him.

"You invited her?" Melinda asked, surveying Parker with huge, wounded eyes.

"She invited herself." He forced himself upright and started propelling himself forward.

"Are—are you all right?" Melinda asked.

"Just dandy," he snapped, unable to keep the cynicism from his voice. "I think we'd all better go into the house, and straighten out a few things." He glanced over his shoulder to Shawna, who was attempting to comb the tangles from her hair with her fingers. "Coming, Doctor?"

"Wouldn't miss it for the world," she quipped back, managing a smile though her insides were shredding. What would she do if he threw her out, insisted that he cared about Melinda, that the child was his?

"One step at a time," she reminded herself, following him inside.

Melinda was already halfway down the hall to the den. "I don't like this," Shawna confided in Parker as she caught up with him.

"Neither do I." His gaze wandered to her face and she could feel his eyes taking in the determined slant of her mouth. "But then there's a lot of things I don't like—things I'm not sure about."

"Such as?"

Before she could walk down the two steps to the den, he leaned forward, balanced on his crutches, and touched her shoulder. "Such as you," he admitted, eyes dark and tormented. "It would be easy to fall in love with you, Shawna—too easy. I must have been one helluva lucky guy—"

"You still are."

"—but now, things have changed. Look at me! I still can't walk. I may never walk without these infernal things!" He shook one crutch angrily, his expression changing to violent anger and frustration. "And then there's Melinda. I can't say her story isn't true. I don't know! I can't remember."

"I'll help you."

He let out a weary sigh and rested his forehead against hers. Involuntarily her fingers caught in the thick threads of his sweater. So desperately, she wanted him to understand, remember, recapture that fleeting love they'd shared.

One of his hands stroked her cheek, as if he couldn't quite believe she was real. "You—you've got a medical practice—a future, and you're a gorgeous, intelligent woman. Any man would count himself lucky if you just looked sideways at him."

"I'm not interested in 'any man,'" she pointed out. "Just one."

"Oh, Shawna," he moaned, his voice as low as the wind rustling through the rafters of the old house. Against her cheek, his fingers trembled.

A hot lump filled her throat. "How come I feel like you're trying to push me away?"

"Because I am. I have to. I can't tie you down to this!" He gestured to his legs, furious that they wouldn't obey his commands.

"Let me make that decision." Tears filled her eyes, but she smiled bravely just the same. "I'll decide if you're so horrible that any sane woman wouldn't be interested in you."

From the doorway to the den, Melinda coughed. She glanced guiltily away, as if she didn't mean to eavesdrop, but hadn't been able to stop herself from witnessing the tender scene between Parker and Shawna. "If you want me to, I'll leave," she said, chin quivering.

"Not yet." Straightening, Parker rubbed one hand around his shoulders, as if to relieve a coiled tension in his muscles. "Not yet." He swung his crutches forward and hobbled down the two steps into the den.

Steeling herself, Shawna followed, only to find that Melinda had already lit a fire in the grate and had placed a carafe of coffee on the table. "You've been here a while."

Melinda shrugged but resentment smoldered in her large brown eyes. "I, um, didn't expect you."

Parker met the questions in Melinda's gaze. "I think we'd better set a few ground rules. First of all, I don't remember you, not in the way you think I should," he said to Melinda. "But, if that child is really mind, I'll do right by you."

"That's all I'd expect," Melinda replied quickly. "I'm just concerned for my baby."

Shawna's hands shook. Just thinking that Parker might have a child with someone else, even a child conceived before they had met, tore at her soul. I can handle this, she told herself over and over again, trying to convince herself.

"Okay, so how did we meet?" Parker said, leaning forward and cringing a little when a jab of pain shot through him.

"I—I was a friend of Brad's. I, uh, used to watch him play and you coached him. Brad—he introduced us."

"How did you know Brad?"

Melinda looked down at her hands. "We went to school together in Cleveland, before he dropped out," she explained. "We, uh, used to date."

"But then you met Parker," Shawna prodded.

"Yes, and, well, Brad was seeing someone else, Parker and I hit it off, and then," she licked her lips. "We fell in love. Until you came along."

Shawna exhaled slowly. How much of Melinda's story was fact and how much fantasy? If only Parker could remember! She wanted to hate the girl but couldn't. Melinda was afraid of something, or someone; it was written all over her downcast face.

"Do you have any family?" Parker asked.

"Not around here. My dad's a widower."

"Does he know that you're pregnant?"

"I didn't know until I saw *her* yesterday," Melinda said, then her shoulders slumped. "Though I guess I kinda expected it. But Dad, even if he did know, he wouldn't care. I haven't lived at home for a couple of years."

"I thought you said he'd kill you," Shawna whispered.

"I guess I was wrong." Melinda swallowed hard and Shawna almost felt sorry for her. "Look, I made a mistake. It's no big deal," she said, her temper flaring. "The thing is I'm in trouble, okay? And it's *his* fault. You know I'm not lying, you're the one who did the test."

Shawna slowly counted to ten. She couldn't lose her self-control. Not now. "Fine. Let's start over."

"I didn't come here to talk to you."

"This involves all of us," Parker said.

Shawna asked, "Did you finish high school?"

"Yep." Melinda flopped onto one of the cushions of the leather couch and stared at the ceiling. "I was going to be a model. Until I met Parker."

"After Brad."

"Right."

Shawna wondered how much, if any, of the girl's story were true. "And then you were swept off your feet?"

"That's about it," Melinda said, her smile faltering.

Parker's expression was unreadable. He stared at Melinda, his lips pressed together, as if he, too, were trying to find flaws in her words, some key to what had really happened. "Then you won't mind if I have a friend of mine look up your father, just to verify a few things," Parker said slowly.

Beneath her tan, Melinda blanched, but said, "Do what you have to do. It won't change anything, and at least then maybe she'll believe me." Disturbed, she slung her purse over her shoulder and left, the heels of her boots echoing loudly on the tiles of the foyer. A few seconds later Shawna heard the front door slam.

"Does anything she said sound true?" she asked.

"I don't know." Parker sighed heavily and, groaning, pushed himself to his feet. "I just don't know." Leaning one shoulder against the stones of the fireplace, he stared into the glowing red embers of the fire. "But she seemed pretty sure of herself. That seems to be a trait of the women I knew."

The firelight flickered on his face, causing uneven red shadows to highlight the hard angle of his jaw. He added, "You know you can't stay here."

"I have to."

"You don't owe me any debts, if that's what you think."

"You need someone to look after you."

"Like hell!" he muttered, his eyes blazing with the reflection of the coals. "What I don't need is any one who thinks they owe me."

"You just don't understand, do you?" she whispered, so furious she was beginning to shake again. "You just don't understand how much I love you."

"Loved. Past tense."

Standing, she tossed her hair away from her face and met his fierce, uncompromising stare. "One accident doesn't change the depth of my feelings, Parker. Nor does it, in any way, shape or form, alter the fact that I love you for life, no matter what. Legally, I suppose, you can force me out of here. Or, you could make my life here so intolerable that I'd eventually throw in the towel and move. But you can't, *can't* destroy the simple fact that I love you and always will." Into the silence that followed, she said, "I've made up the guest room for you so you won't have to hassle with the stairs. I've moved all of your clothes and things down here."

"And you—where do you intend to sleep?"

"Upstairs—for now. Just until this Melinda thing is straightened out."

"And then?"

"Then, I hope, you'll want me to sleep with you."

"As man and wife?"

"Yes. If I can ever get it through that thick skull of yours that we belong together! So," she added fiercely, "if we're finished arguing, I'll make dinner." Leaving him speechless, she marched out of the room, fingers crossed, hoping that somehow, some way, she could help him remember everything.

Parker stared after her in amazement. Nothing was going as he'd planned. Ever since she'd bulldozed her way back into his life, he seemed to have lost control—not only of his past, but of his future.

Unfortunately he admired her grit and determination, and even smiled to himself when he remembered how emphatic she'd become when she'd told him she intended to sleep with him. Any other man would jump at the chance of making love to her—but then any other man could jump and make love. So far he hadn't done either since the accident. He was sure he couldn't do one. As for the other, he hoped that he was experiencing only a temporary setback. He smiled a little. Earlier, when he'd fallen on the ground and he'd kissed Shawna, he'd felt the faintest of stirrings deep within.

Now, he found his crutches and pushed himself down the hallway toward the kitchen. Shawna was so passionate, so full of life. Why would he betray her with a woman who was barely out of childhood?

He leaned one shoulder against the wall and watched Shawna working in the kitchen. She'd tied a towel over her wool skirt, clipped her hair loosely away from her face, and kicked her shoes into a corner. In stocking feet and reading glasses, she sliced vegetables near the sink. She was humming— actually humming—as she worked, and she seemed completely at home and comfortable in his house, as though their argument and Melinda's baby didn't exist.

Watching her furtively, listening to the soft sound of her voice, seeing the smile playing upon her lips, he couldn't help feeling as lighthearted as she. She was a beautiful, intriguing woman—a woman with determination and courage—and she gave her love to him so completely.

So how could he have betrayed her? Deep inside, he knew he wouldn't have cheated on her. Yet he couldn't dismiss the fact that he vaguely remembered Melinda James.

She glanced up sharply, as if sensing him for the first time, and she blushed. "I didn't hear you."

"It's okay, I was just watching."

"Well, come in and take a center seat. No reason to hide in the hall," she teased.

Parker grinned and hobbled into the kitchen where he half fell into one of the caned chairs. "Don't let me disturb you," he said.

"Wouldn't dream of it!" She pushed her glasses onto the bridge of her nose and continued reading a recipe card. "You're in for the thrill of your life," she declared. "*Coq au vin* à la Shawna. This is going to be great."

"I know," he admitted, folding his arms over his chest, propping his bad leg on a nearby chair, and grinning to himself. Great it would be, but he wasn't thinking about the chicken in wine.

Nine

Shawna eyed the dining room table critically. It gleamed with a fresh coat of wax and reflected the tiny flames of two creamy white candles. She'd polished the brass candlesticks and placed a fresh bouquet of roses and baby's breath between the flickering candles.

Tonight, whether Parker was agreeable or not, they were going to celebrate. She'd been living with him for over three weeks in a tentative truce. Fortunately, Melinda hadn't intruded, though Parker had spoken with her on the phone several times.

"Buck up," she told herself, as she thought about the girl. Melinda was pregnant and they couldn't ignore her. Even though neither she nor Parker had brought up the subject of Melinda's baby, it was always in the air, and invisible barrier between them.

In the past weeks, Parker had spent his days in physical therapy, either at Mercy Hospital or here, at the house.

Shawna rearranged one drooping flower and frowned. As a doctor, she knew that Parker was pushing himself to the limit, forcing muscles and ligaments to work, as if regaining full use of his leg would somehow trip his memory. Though Shawna had begged him to slow down, he'd refused to listen, mule-headedly driving himself into a state of utter exhaustion.

Finally, at the end of the third week, he'd improved to the point that he was walking with only the aid of a cane.

To celebrate, she'd taken the afternoon off and had been waiting for him, cooking and cleaning and feeling nearly as if she belonged in his house—almost as if she were his wife.

She heard his car in the drive. Smiling, she hurried into the kitchen to add the last touches to the beef stroganoff simmering on the stove.

Parker opened the back door and collapsed into one of the kitchen chairs. His hair was dark with sweat and his face was gaunt and strained as he hung his cane over the back of his chair. He winced as he lifted his bad leg and propped it on a stool. Glancing up, he forced a tired smile. "Hi."

Shawna leaned over the counter separating kitchen from nook. "Hi, yourself."

"I thought you had the late shift."

"I traded so that we could have dinner together," she said.

"Sounds good." But he really wasn't listening. He was massaging his knee, his lips tightening as his fingers touched a particularly sensitive spot.

"You've been pushing yourself too hard again," she said softly, worried that he would do himself more damage than good.

"I don't think so."

"I'm a doctor."

He rolled his eyes. "Don't I know it?"

"Parker, please," she said, kneeling in front of him and placing a kiss on his sweat-dampened forehead. "Take it easy."

"I can't."

"There's plenty of time—"

"Do you really believe that?" He was staring at her suspiciously, as if he thought she was lying to him.

"You've got the rest of your—"

"Easy for you to say, *doctor*," he snapped. "You're not facing the rest of your life with this!" He lifted his cane, then, furious with the damned thing, hurled it angrily across the room. It skidded on the blue tiles and smashed into a far wall.

Shawna wanted to lecture him, but didn't. Instead she straightened and pretended interest in the simmering sauce. "I, uh, take it the session wasn't the best."

"You take it right, doctor. But then you know everything, don't you?" He gestured toward the stove. "What I should eat, where I should sleep, how fast I should improve—all on your neat little schedule!"

His words stung and she gasped, before stiffening her back and pretending he hadn't wounded her. The tension between them had been mounting for weeks. He was disappointed, she told herself.

But he must have recognized her pain. He made a feeble gesture of apology with his hand, then, bracing his palms on the table, forced himself upright.

"I wish things were different," he finally said, gripping the counter with both hands, "but they're not. You're a good woman, Shawna—better than I deserve. Do yourself a favor and forget about me. Find yourself a whole man."

"I have," she whispered, her throat swollen tight. "He's just too pigheaded to know it."

"I mean it—"

"And so do I," she whispered. "I love you, Parker. I always will. That's just the way it is."

He stared at her in amazement, then leaned back, propping his head against the wall. "Oh, God," he groaned, covering his face with his hands. "You live in such a romantic dream world." When he dropped his hands, his expression had changed to a mask of indifference.

"If I live in a dream world," she said quietly, "it's a world that you created."

"Then it's over," he decided, straightening. "It's just . . . gone. It vanished that night."

Shawna ignored the stab of pain in her heart. "I don't believe you and I won't. Until you're completely well and have regained all of your memory, I won't give up."

"Shawna—"

"Remember that 'for better or worse' line?"

"We didn't get married."

Yet, she thought wildly. "Doesn't matter. In my heart I'm committed to you, and only when you tell me that you remember everything we shared and it means nothing to you—then I'll give up!"

"I just don't want to hurt you," he admitted, "ever again."

"You won't." The lie almost caught on her tongue.

"I wish I was as sure as you."

Her heart squeezed as she studied him, his body drenched in sweat, his shoulder balanced precariously against the wall.

As if reading the pity in her eyes, he swore, anger darkening his face. Casting her a disbelieving glance, he limped down the hall to his room and slammed the door so hard that the sound echoed through the old house.

Shawna stared after him. Why couldn't he remember how strong their love had been? *Why?* Feeling the need to break down and cry like a baby, she steeled herself. In frustration, she reached for the phone, hoping to call her brother or her friend Gerri or anyone to whom she could vent her frustrations. But when she placed the receiver to her ear, she heard Parker on the bedroom extension.

"That's right . . . everything you can find out about her. The name's James—Melinda James. I don't know her middle name. She claims to have been living in Cleveland and that she grew up with Brad Lomax."

Quietly, Shawna replaced the receiver. It seemed that no matter where she turned or how fiercely she clung to the ashes of the love she and Parker had once shared, the winds of fate blew them from her fingers. Dying a little inside, she wondered if he was right. Maybe the flames of their love couldn't be rekindled.

"Give him time," she told herself, but she knew their time was running out. She glanced around the old Tudor house, the home she'd planned to share with him. She'd moved in, but they were both living a lie. He didn't love her.

Swallowing against the dryness in her throat, she turned toward the sink and ran water over the spinach leaves in a colander. She ignored the tears that threatened to form in the corners of her eyes. *Don't give up!* part of her insisted, while the other, more reasonable side of her nature whispered, *Let him go.*

So intent was she on tearing spinach, cutting egg, and crumbling bacon that she didn't hear the uneven tread of his footsteps in the hall, didn't feel his gaze on her back as she worked, still muttering and arguing with herself.

Her first indication that he was in the room with her was the feel of his hands on her waist. She nearly dropped her knife as he bent his head and rested his chin on her shoulder.

"I'm not much good at apologies," he said softly.

"Neither am I."

"Oh, Shawna." His breath fanned her hair, warm and enticing, and her heart took flight. He'd come back! "I know you're doing what you think is best," he said huskily. "And I appreciate your help."

She dropped the knife and the tears she'd been fighting filled her eyes. "I've done it because I want to."

His fingers spanned her waist. "I just don't understand," he admitted, "why you want to put up with me."

She wanted to explain, but he cut her off, his arms encircling her waist, her body drawn to his. His breath was hot on the back of her head and delicious shivers darted along her spine as he pulled her close, so close that her back was pressed against the taut muscles of his chest. A spreading warmth radiated to her most outer limbs as his lips found her nape.

"I—I love you, Parker."

His muscles flexed and she silently prayed he would return those three simple words.

"That's why I'm working so hard," he conceded, his voice rough with emotion. "I want to be able to remember everything."

"I can wait," she said.

"But I can't! I want my life back—all of it. The way it was before the accident. Before—"

He didn't say it, but she knew. *Before Brad was killed, before Melinda James shattered our lives.*

"Maybe we should eat," she said, hoping to divert him from the guilt that ran rampant every time he thought about Brad.

"You've worked hard, haven't you?"

"It's a—well, it was a celebration."

"Oh?"

"Because you're off crutches and out of the brace," she said.

"I've still got that." He pointed to where the cane still lay on the floor.

"I know, but it's the final step."

"Except for my memory."

"It'll come back," she predicted, sounding more hopeful than she felt. "Come on, now," she urged. "Make yourself useful. Pour the wine before I ruin dinner and the candles burn out."

During dinner Shawna felt more lighthearted than she had in weeks. At the end of the meal, when Parker leaned forward and brushed his lips over hers, she thought fleetingly that together they could face anything.

"Thanks," he whispered, "for putting up with me."

"I wouldn't have it any other way." She could feel her eyes shining in the candlelight, knew her cheeks were tinged with the blush of happiness.

"Let's finish this—" he said, holding the wine bottle by its neck, "—in the gazebo."

A dimple creased her cheek. "The gazebo?" she repeated, and grinned from ear to ear as she picked up their wine glasses and dashed to the hallway where her down coat hung. Her heart was pounding with excitement. Just two months earlier, Parker had proposed in the gazebo.

Hand in hand, they walked down a flagstone path that led to the river. The sound of water rushing over stones filled the night air and a breeze fresh with the scent of the Willamette lifted Shawna's hair.

The sky was clear and black. A ribbon of silver moonlight rippled across the dark water to illuminate the bleached wood and smooth white rocks at the river's edge. On the east bank, lights from neighboring houses glittered and reflected on the water.

Shawna, with Parker's help, stepped into the gazebo. The slatted wood building was built on the edge of Parker's property, on the ridge overlooking the Willamette. The gazebo was flanked by lilac bushes, no longer fragrant, their dry leaves rustling in the wind.

As Shawna stared across the water, she felt Parker's arms slip around her waist, his breath warm against her head, the heat from his body flowing into hers.

"Do—do you remember the last time we were here?" she whispered, her throat swollen with the beautiful memory.

He didn't say anything.

"You proposed," she prodded.

"Did I?"

"Yes." She turned in his arms, facing him. "Late in the summer."

Squinting his eyes, fighting the darkness shrouding his brain, he struggled, but nothing surfaced. "I'm sorry," he whispered, his night-darkened eyes searching hers.

"Don't apologize," she whispered. Moonlight shifted across his face, shadowing the sharp angles as he lowered his head and touched his lips to hers.

Gently, his fingers twined in her hair. "Sometimes I get caught up in your fantasies," he admitted, his lips twisting cynically.

"This isn't a fantasy," she said, seeing her reflection in his eyes. "Just trust me."

He leaned forward again, brushing his lips suggestively over hers. "That's the trouble. I do." He took the wine and glasses and set them on the bench. Placing his palms on her cheeks, he stared into her eyes before kissing her again. Eagerly she responded, her heart pulsing wildly at his touch, her mouth opening willingly to the erotic pressure of his tongue on her lips.

She felt his hands quiver as they slid downward to rest near her neck, gently massaging her nape, before pushing the coat from her shoulders. The night air surrounded her, but she wasn't cold.

Together, they slid slowly to the weathered floorboards and Parker adjusted her down coat, using its softness as a mattress. Then, still kissing her, he found the buttons of her blouse and loosened them, slipping the soft fabric down her shoulders.

Slowly he bent and pressed his moist lips against the base of her throat.

In response, she warmed deep within, stretching her arms around him, holding him tight, drinking in the smell and feel of him.

"Shawna," he whispered.

"Oh, Parker, love," she murmured.

"Tell me to stop."

"Don't ever stop," she cried.

He shuddered, as if trying to restrain himself,

then, in one glorious minute, he crushed his lips to hers and kissed her more passionately than ever before. His hands caressed her skin, tearing at her blouse and the clasp of her bra, baring her breasts to the shifting moonlight. Slowly he lowered his head and touched each proud nipple with his lips, teasing the dark peaks to impatient attention.

"Ooh," she whispered, caught up in the warm, rolling sensations of his lips and tongue as he touched her, stoking fires that scorched as they raced through her blood and burned wantonly in her brain.

Reckless desire chased all rational thought away.

Her breath tangled with his and his hands touched her, sweeping off her skirt until she was naked in the night. Her skin was as white as alabaster in the darkness. Despite the cool river-kissed wind, she was warm deep inside, as she throbbed with need for this one special man.

His moist lips moved over her, caressing her, arousing her, stealing over her skin and causing her mind to scream with the want of him.

She found the hem of his sweater and pushed the offending garment over his head. He groaned in response and she unsnapped his jeans, her fingers sliding down the length of his legs as she removed the faded denim until, at last, they lay naked in the tiny gazebo—his body gleaming with a dewy coat of sweat, hers rosy with the blush of desire.

"I will always love you," she promised as he lowered himself over her, twisting his fingers in her hair, his eyes blue lusting flames.

"And I'll always love you," he vowed into her open mouth as his hands closed over her breasts, gently kneading the soft, proud nipples, still wet from his kiss.

Her fingers moved slowly down his back, touching firm smooth muscles and the gentle cleft of his spine.

Though her eyes wanted to close, she willed them open, staring up at him, watching the bittersweet torment on his face as he delved inside, burying himself in her only to withdraw again and again. Her heart slamming wildly, her blood running molten hot, she arched upward, moved by a primitive force and whispering words of love.

Caught in her own storm of emotion and the powerful force of his love, she lost herself to him, surrendering to the vibrant spinning world that was theirs alone. She felt the splendor of his hands, heard him cry out her name.

In one glorious moment he stiffened, his voice reverberating through the gazebo and out across the river, and Shawna, too, convulsed against his sweat-glistened body.

His breath was rapid and hot in her ear. "This . . . could be dangerous," he whispered hoarsely, running a shaking hand through his hair.

Still wrapped in the wonder and glow of passion, she held him close, pressed her lips to his sweat-soaked chest. "Don't talk. For just tonight, let's pretend that it's only you and me, and our love."

"I'm not much good at pretending." Glancing down at her plump breasts, he sighed, then reached past her to a glass on the bench. Swirling wine in the goblet, he said, "I don't think we should let this happen again."

"I don't think we have a choice."

"Oh, Shawna," he whispered, drinking his wine and setting the empty glass on the floor before he reached behind her, to wrap the coat over her suddenly chilled shoulders before holding her close. "This isn't a question of love," he said.

Crushed, she couldn't answer.

"I just think we both need time."

"Because of Melinda's baby."

"The baby has something to do with it," he admitted, propping himself against the bench. He drew her draped body next to his and whispered against her neck. "But there's more. I don't want to tie you down."

"But you're not—"

"Shh. Just listen. I'm not the man you were in love with before the accident. Too much has changed for us to be so naive to think that everything will be just as we'd planned, which, for the record, I still can't remember."

"You will, " she said, though she felt a gaping hole in her heart.

Parker slid from behind her and reached for his clothes. He'd never intended to make love to her, to admit that he loved her, for crying out loud, but there it was—the plain simple truth: He loved her and he couldn't keep his hands off her.

"I think I'll go for a drive," he said, yanking his sweater over his head and sliding with difficulty into his jeans.

"Now?"

"I need time to think, Shawna. We both do," he said abruptly. Seeing the wounded look in her eyes he touched her cheek. "You know I care about you," he admitted, stroking her hair. "But I need a little space, just to work things out. I don't want either of us to make a mistake we'll regret later."

"Maybe we already have," she said, clutching her coat over her full breasts. She lifted her chin bravely, though deep inside, she was wounded to the core.

Just minutes before he was loving her, now he was walking away!

"Maybe," he groaned, then straightened and hobbled to the door.

Shawna watched him amble up the path and shuddered when she heard the garage door slam behind him. He was gone. It was that simple. Right after making love to her for the first time, he'd walked away. The pain in her heart throbbed horribly, though she tried to believe that his words of love, sworn in the throes of passion, were the only real truth.

Brittle night wind raced through the car as Parker drove, his foot on the throttle, the windows rolled down. He pushed the speed limit, needing the cold night air to cool the passion deep in his soul. He was rocked to his very core by the depth of his feelings for Shawna. Never would he have believed himself capable of such all-consuming physical and mental torture. He wanted her—forever. He'd been on the verge of asking her to marry him back in the gazebo and damning the consequences.

"You're a fool," he chastised, shifting down, the car squealing around a curve in the road. Lights in the opposite lane dazzled and blinded him, bore down on him. "A damned fool."

The car in the oncoming lane passed, and memories crashed through the walls of his blocked mind. One by one they streamed into his consciousness. He remembered Brad, passed out and unconscious, and Melinda crying softly, clinging to Parker's shoulder. And Shawna—Lord, he remembered her, but not as he saw her now. Yes, he'd loved her because she was a beautiful intelligent woman, but in the past, he hadn't felt this overpowering awe and voracious need that now consumed him.

He strained to remember everything, but couldn't. "Give it time," he said impatiently, but his fingers tightened over the wheel and he felt a desperate desire to know everything.

"Come on, come on," he urged, then realized that he was speeding, as if running from the black hole that was his past.

With difficulty, he eased up on the throttle and drove more cautiously, his hot blood finally cooled. Making love to Shawna had been a mistake, he decided, though a smile of satisfaction still hovered over his lips at the thought of her ivory-white body stretched sensually in the gazebo, her green eyes luminous with desire.

"Forget it," he muttered, palms suddenly damp. Until he remembered everything and knew she loved the man he was today, not the person she'd planned to marry before the accident, he couldn't risk making love to her again.

And that, he thought, his lips twisting wryly, was a crying shame.

Ten

"He's pushing too hard," Bob Killingsworth, Parker's physical therapist, admitted to Shawna one afternoon. She had taken the day off and had intended to spend it with Parker, but he was still in his indoor pool, swimming, using the strength of his arms to pull himself through the water. Though one muscular leg kicked easily, the other, the knee that had been crushed, was stiff and inflexible and dragged noticeably.

"That's it!" Bob called, cupping his hands around his mouth and shouting at Parker.

Parker stood in the shallow end and rubbed the water from his face. "Just a couple more laps."

Glancing at his watch, Bob frowned. "I've got to get to the hospital—"

"I don't need a keeper," Parker reminded him.

"It's all right," Shawna whispered, "I'll stay with him."

"Are you sure?"

"I *am* a doctor."

"I know, but—" Bob shrugged his big shoulders. "Whatever you say."

As Bob left, Shawna kicked off her shoes.

"Joining me?" Parker mocked.

"I just might." The tension between them crackled. Since he'd left her the night they had made love, they had barely spoken. With an impish grin, she slid quickly out of her panty hose and sat on the edge of the pool near the diving board, her legs dangling into the water.

"That looks dangerous, Doctor," Parker predicted from the shallow end.

"I doubt it."

"Oh?" Smothering a devilish grin, Parker swam rapidly toward her, his muscular body knifing through the water. She watched with pride. In two weeks, he'd made incredible strides, physically if not mentally.

He'd always been an athlete and his muscles were strident and powerful. His shoulders were wide, his chest broad and corded. His abdomen was flat as it disappeared inside his swimming trunks to emerge again in the form of lean hips and strong legs— well, at least one strong leg. His right knee was still ablaze with angry red scars.

As he reached the deep end of the pool, he surfaced and his incredible blue eyes danced mischievously. He tossed his hair from his face and water sprayed on her blouse.

"What's on your mind?" she asked, grinning.

"I thought you were coming in."

"And I thought I'd change first."

"Did you?" One side of his mouth lifted into a crafty grin.

"Oh, Parker, no—" she said, just as she felt strong hands wrap over her ankles. "You wouldn't—"

But he did. Over her protests, he gently started swimming backward, pulling her off her bottom and into the pool, wool skirt, silk blouse, and all.

"You're despicable!" she sputtered, surfacing, her hair drenched.

"Probably."

"And cruel and . . . and heartless . . . and—"

"Adorable," he cut in, laughing so loudly the rich sound echoed on the rafters over the pool. His hands had moved upward over her legs, to rest at her hips as she hung by the tips of her fingers at the edge of the pool.

"That, too," she admitted, lost in his eyes as he studied her. Heart pounding erratically, she could barely breathe as his head lowered and his lips brushed erotically over hers.

"So are you." One strong arm gripped her tighter, so fierce and possessive that her breath was trapped somewhere between her throat and lungs, while he clung to the side of the pool with his free hand. "Oh, so are you."

Knowing she was playing with proverbial fire, she warned herself to leave, but she was too caught up in the wonder of being held by him, the feel of his wet body pressed against hers, to consider why his feelings had changed. She didn't care that her clothes were ruined. She'd waited too long for this glorious moment—to have him hold her and want her again.

His tongue rimmed her mouth before parting her lips insistently. Moaning her surrender she felt his mouth crush against hers, his tongue touch and glide with hers, delving delicately then flicking away as she ached for more. Her blood raced uncontrollably, and her heart hammered crazily against her ribs.

She didn't know why he had chosen this moment to love her again. She could only hope that he'd somehow experienced a breakthrough with his memory and could remember everything—especially how much they had loved each other.

His warm lips slid lower on her neck to the base of her throat and the white skin exposed between the lapels of her soggy blouse. The wet silk clung to her, and her nipples, proudly erect, were visible beneath the thin layer of silk and lace, sweetly enticing just above the lapping water.

Lazily, as if he had all the time in the world, his tongue touched her breast, hot as it pressed against her skin. She cried out, couldn't help herself, as he slowly placed his mouth against her, nuzzling her, sending white-hot rivulets of desire through her veins.

She could only cling to him, holding his head against her breast, feeling the warmth within her start to glow and a dull ache begin to throb deep at her center.

She didn't resist as with one hand he undid the buttons of her blouse, baring her shoulders, and letting the sodden piece of silk drift downward into the clear depths of the pool. Her bra, a flimsy scrap of lace, followed.

She was bare from the waist up, her breasts straining and full beneath his gaze as clear water lapped against her white skin.

"You are so beautiful," he groaned, as if her beauty were a curse. He gently reached forward, softly stroking her skin, watching in fascination as her nipple tightened, his eyes devouring every naked inch of her skin. "This is crazy, absolutely crazy," he whispered. Then, almost angrily, he lifted her up and took one bare nipple into his mouth, feasting hungrily on the soft white globe, his hand against her back, causing goose bumps to rise on her skin.

"Love me," she cried, aching to be filled with his spirit and soul. Her hands tangled in the hair of his chest and her eyes glazed as she whispered, "Please, Parker, make love to me."

"Right here?" he asked, lifting his head, short of breath.

"I don't care . . . anywhere."

His lips found hers again and as he kissed her, feeling her warm body in the cool water, a jagged piece of memory pricked his mind. Hadn't there been another time, another place, when Shawna—or had it been another woman—had pleaded with him to make love to her?

The sun had been hot and heat shimmered in vibrant waves over the river. They were lying in a canoe, the boat rocking quietly as he'd kissed her, his heart pounding in his ears, her suntanned body molded against his. She'd whispered his name, her voice rough with longing, then . . .

Just as suddenly as the memory had appeared, it slipped away again.

"Parker?"

He blinked, finding himself in the pool with Shawna, her green eyes fixed on his, her white skin turning blue in the suddenly-cold water.

"What is it?"

"I don't know," he admitted, frustrated all over again. If only he could remember! If only he could fill the holes in his life! He released her and swam to the edge of the pool. "I think maybe you'd better get dressed," he decided, hoisting his wet body out of the water and reaching for a towel. "I—I'm sorry about your clothes."

"No—"

But he was already limping toward the door.

Dumbfounded, she dived for her blouse and bra, struggled into them, and surfaced at the shallow end. "You've got a lot of nerve," she said, breathing rapidly, her pride shattered as she climbed, dripping out of the pool. "What was *that*?" Gesturing angrily, she encompassed the entire high-ceilinged room to include the intimacy they'd just shared.

"A mistake," he said, wincing a little. Snatching his cane from a towel rack, he turned to the door.

"Mistake?" she yelled. "Mistake?" Boiling, her female ego trampled upon one too many times, she caught up to him and placed herself, with her skirt and blouse still dripping huge puddles on the concrete, squarely in his path. "Just like the other night was a mistake?"

His gaze softened. "I told you—we need time."

But she wasn't listening. "I know what you're doing," she said, pointing an accusing finger at him. "You're trying to shame me into leaving!"

"That's ridiculous!"

"Is it? Then explain what that scene in the pool was all about! We nearly made love, for crying out loud, and now you're walking out of here as if nothing happened. Just like the other night! That's it, isn't it? You're trying to mortify me!" All her pent-up emotions exploded, and without thinking she slapped him, her palm smacking as it connected with his jaw. The sound reverberated through the room.

"Thank you, Dr. McGuire," he muttered, his temper erupting. "Once again your bedside manner is at its finest!" Without another word he strode past her, limping slightly as he yanked open the door and slammed it shut behind him.

Shawna slumped against the brick wall. She felt as miserable and bedraggled as she looked in her wet clothes. Stung by his bitterness and the cruelty she'd seen in his gaze, she closed her eyes, feeling the cold of the bricks permeate her damp clothes. Had he set her up on purpose? Her head fell to her hands. Had he planned to make love to her only to throw her aside, in order to wound her and get her out of his life? "Bastard!" she cursed, flinging her wet hair over her shoulder.

Maybe she should leave. Maybe there was no chance of ever recovering what they had lost. Maybe, just maybe, their love affair was truly over. Sick at heart, she sank down against the wall and huddled in a puddle of water near the door.

Then her fists clenched tightly and she took a long, steadying breath. She wouldn't give up—not yet, because she believed in their love. She just had to get him to see things her way!

Parker slammed his bedroom door and uttered a quick oath. What had he been thinking about back there in the pool? Why had he let her get to him that way? He yanked off his wet swim trunks and threw them into a corner.

Muttering to himself, he started to struggle into a pair of old jeans when the door to his room swung open and Shawna, managing to hold her head high though her clothes were wet and dripping and her hair hung lankily around her face, said, "You've got company."

"I don't want—"

"Too late. She's here."

"She?" he repeated, seeing the pain in her eyes.

"Melinda. She's waiting in the den."

Parker zipped up his jeans, aware of her gaze following his movements. He didn't care, he told himself, didn't give one damn what she thought. Grabbing a T-shirt and yanking it over his head, he frowned and made a sound of disgust. "What's she doing here?" he finally asked, holding onto the rails of the bed as he hobbled toward the door.

"Your guess is as good as mine, but I don't think I'll stick around to find out. You know the old saying, three's a crowd."

He watched as she marched stiffly upstairs. He could hear her slamming drawers and he cringed as he made his way to the den.

Melinda was there all right. Standing next to the windows, she straightened as he entered. "So Shawna's still here," she said without any trace of inflection.

"So far."

"And she's staying?" Melinda asked, not meeting his eyes.

"That remains to be seen." He flinched as he heard Shawna stomping overhead. A light fixture rattled in the ceiling. Cocking his head toward an old rocker, he said, "Have a seat."

"No. I'm not staying long. I just came to find out what you intend to do—about the baby, I mean. You do remember, don't you? About the baby?"

Sighing wearily, he stretched his bad leg in front of him and half fell onto the raised hearth of the fireplace. The stones were cold and dusty with ash, but he couldn't have cared less. "What do you want to do?" he asked.

"I don't know." Her chin quivered a little and she chewed on her lower lip. "I suppose you want me to have an abortion."

His skin paled and he felt as if she'd just kicked him in the stomach. "No way. There are lots of alternatives. Abortion isn't one."

She closed her eyes. "Good," she whispered, obviously relieved as she wrapped her arms around herself. "So what about us?"

"Us?"

"Yes—you and me."

He heard Shawna stomp down the stairs and slam the front door shut behind her. Glancing out the window, he saw her, head bent against the wind as she ran to her car. Suddenly he felt as cold as the foggy day.

"Parker?"

He'd almost forgotten Melinda and he glanced up swiftly. She stared at him with wounded eyes and it was hard for him to believe she was lying—yet he couldn't remember ever loving her.

"We have a baby on the way." Swallowing hard, she fought tears that began to drizzle down her face and lowered her head, her black hair glossy as it fell over her face. "You still don't believe me," she accused, her voice breaking.

"I don't know what to believe," he admitted. Leaning his head back against the stones, he strained for images of that night. His head began to throb with the effort. Dark pieces emerged. He remembered seeing her that rainy night, thought she'd held him and cried into the crook of his neck. Had he stroked her hair, comforted her? God, if he could only remember!

"You're falling in love with her again," she charged, sniffing, lifting her head. When he didn't answer, she wiped at her eyes and crossed the room. "Don't be fooled, Parker. She'll lie to you, try to make you doubt me. But this," she patted her abdomen, "is proof of our love."

"If it's mine," he said slowly, watching for any sign that she might be lying. A shadow flickered in her gaze—but only for an instant—then her face was set again with rock-solid resolve.

"Just think long and hard about the night before you were supposed to get married, Parker. Where were you before the accident? In whose bed?"

His skin tightened. Surely he hadn't— Eyes narrowing, he stared up at her. "If I was in your bed, where was Brad?" he asked, as memory after painful memory pricked at his conscience only to escape before he could really latch on to anything solid.

"Passed out on the couch," she said bitterly, hiking the strap of her purse over her shoulder. "He'd drunk too much."

He almost believed her. Something about what she was saying was true. He could sense it. "So," he said slowly, "if I'd planned to stay with you that night, why didn't I take Brad home first?"

She paled a bit, then blinked back sudden tears. "Beats me. Look, I'm not trying to hassle you or Shawna. I just took her advice by giving you all the facts."

"And what do you expect to get out of it?" he asked, studying the tilt of her chin.

"Hey, don't get the wrong idea, you don't *have* to marry me—we never had that kind of a deal, but I do want my son to know his father and I would expect you to . . ." She lifted one shoulder. "You know . . . take care of us."

"Financially?"

She nodded, some of her hard edge dissipating. "What happened—the accident and you losing your memory—isn't really fair to the baby, is it?"

"Maybe nothing's fair," he said, then raked his fingers through his hair. He'd never let anyone manipulate him and he had the distinct feeling that Melinda James was doing just that. Scowling, he felt cornered, and he wanted to put her in her place. But he couldn't. No matter what the truth of the matter was, her unborn child hadn't asked to be brought into a world with a teenager for a mother and no father to care for him.

When the phone rang, she stood. "Think about it," she advised, swinging her purse over her shoulder and heading toward the door.

Closing his eyes, he dropped his face into his hands and tried to think, tried to remember sleeping with Melinda, making love to her.

But he couldn't remember anything. Though he strained to concentrate on the dark-haired young woman who claimed to be carrying his child, the image that swam in front of his eyes was the flushed and laughing face of Shawna McGuire as she clung to the neck of a white carousel stallion.

Once again he saw her laughing, her blond hair billowing behind her as she reached, grabbing blindly for a ribboned brass ring. Or was the image caused by looking too long at photographs of that fateful day?

Think, Harrison, think!

A fortune-teller with voluminous skirts sat by a

small table in a foul-smelling tent as she held Shawna's palm. Gray clouds gathered overhead, rain began to pepper the ground, the road was dark and wet, and Brad was screaming. . . .

Parker gritted his teeth, concentrating so much his entire head throbbed. He had to remember. He had to!

The phone rang again, for the fourth or fifth time, and he reached to answer it just in time to hear the smooth voice of Lon Saxon, a friend and private detective. "That you, Parker?"

"Right here," Parker replied.

"Good. I've got some of the information you wanted on Melinda James."

Parker's guts wrenched. Here it was. The story. "Okay, tell me all about her."

Shawna's fingers were clammy on the wheel as she turned into the drive of Parker's house. After driving aimlessly through the damp streets of Portland, she decided she had to return and confront him. She couldn't run from him and Melinda's baby like some wounded animal.

Silently praying that Melinda had already left, Shawna was relieved to see that the girl's tiny convertible wasn't parked in the drive.

"Remember that he loves you," she told herself as she flicked off the engine and picked up the white bags of hamburgers she'd bought at a local fast-food restaurant. "Just give him time."

Inside, the house was quiet, and for a heart-stopping minute, Shawna thought Parker had left with Melinda. The den was dark and cold, the living room empty. Then she noticed a shaft of light streaming from under the door of his bedroom.

She knocked lightly on the panels, then poked her head inside.

He was still dressed in the old jeans but his shirt was hanging limply from a post on the bed, and his chest was stripped bare. His head was propped by huge pillows and he stared straight at her as if he'd never seen her before.

"Truce?" she asked, holding up two white bags of food.

He didn't move, except to shift his gaze to the bags.

"Was it bad? With Melinda?"

"Did you expect it to be good?"

Hanging on to her emotions, she walked into the room and sat on the bed next to him. The mattress sagged a little, but still he didn't move.

Though her hands were trembling, she opened one bag and held out a paper-wrapped burger. When he ignored the offering she set it, along with the white sacks, on the night stand. "I didn't expect anything. Every day has a new set of surprises," she admitted, tossing her hair over her shoulders and staring straight at him, refusing to flinch. "Look, let's be completely honest with each other."

"Haven't we been?"

"I don't know," she admitted. "I—I just don't know where I stand with you any more."

"Then maybe you should move out."

"Maybe," she said slowly, and saw a streak of pain darken his eyes. "Is that what you want?"

"Honesty? Isn't that what you said?"

"Yes." She braced herself for the worst.

His jaw grew rock hard. "Then, *honestly*, I want to do the right thing. If the baby's mine—"

"It isn't," she said.

The look he gave her cut straight through her heart. "Do you know something I don't?"

"No, but—*Yes*. I do know something—something you don't remember—that we loved each other, that we would never have betrayed each other, that Melinda's baby *can't* be yours."

"I remember her," he said softly.

She gave a weak sound of protest.

His throat worked. "And I remember being with her that night—holding her. She was crying and—"

"No! This is all part of her lies!" Shawna screamed, her stomach twisting painfully, her breath constricted and tight. She wanted to lash out and hit anyone or anything that stood in her way. "You're lying to me!"

"Listen to me, damn it!" he said, grabbing her wrist and pulling her forward so that she fell across his chest, her hair spilling over his shoulders. "I remember being with her that night. Everything's not clear, I'll grant you that. But I was in her apartment!"

"Oh, no," she whispered.

"And there's more."

"Parker, please—"

"You were the one who wanted honesty, remember?" His words were harsh, but there wasn't any trace of mockery in his eyes, just blue, searing torment.

"No—"

"Her story checks out, at least part of it. I had a private detective in Cleveland do some digging. Her mother's dead. Her father is an unemployed steelworker who hasn't held a job in ten years! Melinda supported him while she went to high school. He was furious with her when he found out she was pregnant."

Shawna's fingers clenched over the sheets. "That doesn't mean—"

"It means she's not a chronic liar and she obviously has some sense of right and wrong."

"Then we'll just have to wait, won't we?" she asked dully, her entire world black. "Until you regain your memory or the baby's born and paternity tests can be run."

"I don't think so," he said thoughtfully. She didn't move, dread mounting in her heart, knowing the axe was about to fall. "She told me she wants me to recognize the baby as mine and provide support."

"She wants you to marry her, doesn't she? She expects it?"

"No—" he let his voice drop off.

"But you're considering it!" Shawna gasped, all her hopes dashed as the realization struck her. Parker was going to do the noble deed and marry a girl he didn't know! Cold to the bone, she tried to scramble away, but he held her fast. "This is crazy—you *can't* marry her. You don't even remember her!"

"I remember enough," he said, his voice oddly hollow.

For the first time Shawna considered the horrid fact that he might be the baby's father, that he might have betrayed her the week and night before their wedding, had one last fling with a young girl. "I . . . I don't think I want to hear this," she whispered.

"You wanted the truth, Shawna. So here it is: I'm

responsible for Melinda's predicament and I can't ignore that responsibility or pretend it doesn't exist, much as I might want to." His eyes searched her face and she recognized his pain—the bare, glaring fact that he still loved her. She could smell the male- ness of him, hear the beating of his heart, feel the warmth of his skin, and yet he was pushing her away.

"Please, Parker, don't do this—"

"I have no choice."

"You're claiming the baby," she whispered, eyes moist, insides raw and bleeding.

"Yes." His jaw was tight, every muscle in his body rigid as he took in a long, shaky breath. "So—I think it would be better for everyone involved if you moved out."

She closed her eyes as her world began spinning away from her. All her hopes and dreams were just out of reach. She felt his grip slacken. Without a word, she walked to the door. "I—I'll start packing in the morning," she whispered.

"Good."

Then, numb from head to foot, she closed the door behind her. As she slowly mounted the stairs, she thought she heard him swear and then there was a huge crash against one of the walls, as if a fist or object had collided with plaster. But she didn't pay any attention. All she could think about was the horrid emptiness that was her future—a future bar- ren and bleak without Parker.

Eleven

Tossing off the covers, Shawna rolled over and stared at the clock. Three A.M. and the room was pitch black except for the green digital numbers. Tomorrow she was leaving, giving up on Parker.

Before a single tear slid down her cheek, she searched in the darkness for her robe. Her fingers curled in the soft terry fabric and she fought the urge to scream. How could he do this? Why couldn't he remember?

Angry with herself, Parker, and the world in general, she yanked open the door to her room and padded silently along the hall and down the stairs, her fingers trailing on the banister as she moved quietly in the darkness. She didn't want to wake Parker, though she didn't really know why. The thought that he was sleeping peacefully while she was ripped to ribbons inside was infuriating.

In the kitchen she rattled around for a mug, the powdered chocolate, and a carton of milk. Then, while her cocoa was heating in the microwave, she felt a wild need to escape, to run away from the house that trapped her with its painful memories.

Without really thinking she unlocked the French doors of the dining room and walked outside to the balcony overlooking the dark Willamette. The air was fresh and bracing, the sound of the river soothing as it flowed steadily toward the Columbia.

Clouds scudded across a full moon, filtering thin beams of moonlight which battled to illuminate the night and cast shadows on the river. Leaves, caught in the wind, swirled and drifted to the ground.

Shivering, Shawna tightened her belt and leaned forward over the rail, her fingers curling possessively around the painted wood. This house was to have been hers, but losing the house didn't matter. Losing Parker was what destroyed her. She would gladly have lived in a shack with him, if only he could have found his way back to her. But now it was over. Forever.

She heard the microwave beep. Reluctantly she turned, her breath catching in her throat when she found Parker staring at her, one shoulder propped against the open French door.

"Couldn't sleep either?" he asked, his night-darkened gaze caressing her face.

"No." She lifted her chin upward, unaware that moonlight shimmered silver in her hair and reflected in her eyes. "Can I get you a cup?" she asked, motioning toward the kitchen. "Hot chocolate's supposed to do the trick."

"Is that your professional opinion?" For once there was no sarcasm in his voice.

"Well, you know me," she said, laughing bitterly at

the irony. "At least you did. But maybe you don't remember that I don't put too much stock in prescriptions—sleeping pills and the like. Some of the old-fashioned cures are still the best. So, if you want, I'll fix you a cup."

"I don't think so."

Knowing she should leave, just brush past him, grab her damned cocoa and hightail it upstairs, she stood, mesmerized, realizing that this might be their last moment alone. She couldn't help staring pointedly at his bare chest, at his muscles rigid and strident, his jeans riding low over his hips. Nor could she ignore his brooding and thoughtful expression. His angular features were dark and his eyes, what she could see of them, were focused on her face and neck. As his gaze drifted lower to linger at the cleft of her breasts and the wisp of white lace from her nightgown, she swallowed against her suddenly dry throat.

"I thought you should have this," he said quietly as he walked across the balcony, reached into the pocket of his jeans, and extracted the brass ring he'd won at the fair. Even in the darkness she recognized the circle of metal and the ribbons fluttering in the breeze. "You should have caught this that day."

"You remember?" she asked quickly as her fingers touched the cold metal ring.

"Pieces."

Hope sprang exuberantly in her heart. "Then—"

"It doesn't change anything."

"But—"

His hand closed over hers, warm and comforting as his fingers forced hers to curl over the ring. "Take it."

"Parker, please, talk to me!" Desperate, she pleaded with him. "If you remember—then you know the baby—"

His jaw grew rock hard. "I don't know for sure, but you have to accept that the baby is mine," he said, his eyes growing distant. He turned then, limping across the balcony and through the kitchen.

For a few minutes Shawna just stared at the damned ring in her hands as memory after painful memory surfaced. Then, unable to stop herself from trying one last time, she practically flew into the house and down the hall, her bare feet slapping against the wooden floors. "Parker, wait!"

She caught up with him in his bedroom. "Leave it, Shawna," he warned.

"But you remember!" Breathless, her heart hammering, she faced him. "You know what we meant to each other!"

"What I remember," he said coldly, though his gaze said differently, "is that you wouldn't sleep with me."

"We had an agreement," she said weakly, clasping the post of his bed for support. "Maybe it was stupid, but—"

"And you teased me—"

"I what?" But she'd heard the words before. Stricken, she could only whisper, "It was a joke between us. You used to laugh!"

"I told you then you'd drive me to a mistress," he said, his brows pulling down sharply over his eyes.

"You're doing this on purpose," she accused him. "You're forcing yourself to be cruel—just to push me away! All that business about having a mistress . . . you were kidding . . . it was just a little game . . .

oh, God." She swayed against the post. Had she really been so blind? Had Parker and Melinda—? Numb inside she stumbled backward. Before she could say or do anything to further degrade herself, she scrambled out of the room.

"Shawna—"

She heard him call, but didn't listen.

"I didn't mean to—"

But she was already up the stairs, slamming the door shut, embarrassed to tears as she flipped on the light and jerked her suitcases from the closet to fling them open on the bed.

"Damn it, Shawna! Come down here."

No way! She couldn't trust herself, not around him. She wouldn't. She felt close to tears but wouldn't give into them. Instead she flung clothes—dresses, sweaters, underwear, slacks—anything she could find into the first suitcase and slammed it shut.

"Listen to me—"

Dear God, his voice was closer! He was actually struggling up the stairs! What if he fell? What if he lost his balance and stumbled backward! "Leave me alone, Parker!" she shouted, snapping the second suitcase shut. She found her purse, slung the strap over her shoulder, slipped into her shoes, and hauled both bags to the landing.

He was there. His face was red from the exertion of the climb, and his eyes were blazing angrily. "Look," he said, reaching for her, but she spun out of his grasp and he nearly fell backward down the steep stairs.

"Stop it!" she cried, worried sick that he would stumble. "Just stop it!"

"I didn't mean to hurt you—"

"Too late! But it doesn't matter. Not any more. It's over. I'm leaving you alone. That's what you want, isn't it? It's what you've been telling me to do all along. You've got your wish."

"Please—"

Her traitorous heart told her to stay, but this time, damnit, she was going to think with her head. "Good luck, Parker," she choked out. "I mean it, really. I—I wish you the best." Then she ran down the stairs, feeling the tears filling her eyes as she fled through the front door.

The night wind tore at her robe and hair as she raced down the brick path to the garage and the safety of her little hatchback. Gratefully she slid behind the steering wheel and with trembling fingers flicked on the ignition. The engine roared to life just as Parker opened the kitchen door and snapped on the overhead light in the garage.

Shawna sent up a silent prayer of thanks that he'd made it safely downstairs. Then she shoved the gearshift into reverse and the little car squealed out of the garage.

Driving crazily along the empty highway toward Lake Oswego, she could barely breathe. She had to fight to keep from sobbing hysterically as she sought the only safe refuge she knew. Jake—her brother— she could stay with him.

Slow down, she warned herself, as she guided the car toward the south side of the lake where Jake lived in a small bungalow. *Please be home*, she thought as she parked, grabbed her suitcases, and trudged up the front steps to the porch.

The door opened before she could knock and Jake, his dark hair falling in wild locks over his forehead, his jaw stubbled, his eyes bleary, grabbed the heaviest bag. "Come on in, Sis," he said, eyeing her gravely.

"You knew?"

"Parker called. He was worried about you."

She let out a disgusted sound, but when Jake kicked the door shut and wrapped one strong arm around her, she fell apart, letting out the painful sobs that ripped at her soul.

"It's okay," he whispered.

"I wonder if it will ever be," Shawna said, before emitting a long, shuddering sigh and shivering from the cold.

"Come on," Jake suggested, propelling her to the tiny alcove that was his kitchen. "Tell me what happened."

"I don't think I can."

"You don't have much choice. You talk and I'll cook. The best omelet in town."

Shawna's stomach wrenched at the thought of food. "I'm not hungry."

"Well, I am," he said, plopping her down in one of the creaky kitchen chairs and opening the refrigerator. "So, come on, spill it. Just what the hell happened between you and Parker tonight?"

Swallowing hard, Shawna clasped her hands on the table and started at the beginning.

Parker could have kicked himself. Angry with himself, the world, and one lying Melinda James, he ignored the fact that it was the middle of the night and dialed his lawyer.

The phone rang five times before he heard Martin Calloway's groggy voice. "Hello?" he mumbled.

"Hello. This is—"

"I know who it is, Harrison. Do you have any idea what time it is?"

"Vaguely."

"And whatever's on your mind couldn't wait 'til morning?"

"That's about the size of it," Parker said, his gaze roving around the dark, empty kitchen. Damn, but the house felt cold without Shawna. "I want you to draw up some papers."

"Some papers," Martin repeated dryly. "Any particular kind?"

"Adoption," Parker replied flatly, "and post-date them by about six or seven months."

"Wait a minute—what the hell's going on?"

"I've had a breakthrough," Parker said, his entire life crystal clear since his argument with Shawna. "Something happened tonight that brought everything back and now I need to straighten out a few things."

"By adopting a child that isn't born yet?"

"For starters—I don't care how you handle it—I just want to make sure the adoption will be legal and binding."

"I'll need the mother's signature."

"I don't think that will be a problem," Parker said. "Oh—and just one other thing. I want to keep the fact that I'm remembering again a secret."

"Any particular reason?"

"There's someone I have to tell—after we get whatever letters of intent for adoption or whatever it's called signed."

"I'll work on it in the morning."

"Great."

Parker hung up and walked restlessly to his bedroom. He thought about chasing Shawna down at Jake's and admitting that he remembered his past, but decided to wait until everything was settled. This time, he wasn't going to let anything come between them!

If Shawna had known the torment she was letting herself in for, she might have thought twice about leaving Parker so abruptly. Nearly a week had dragged by, one day slipping into the next in a simple routine of patients, hospitals, and sleepless nights. Though Shawna fought depression, it clung to her like a heavy black cloak, weighing down her shoulders and stealing her appetite.

"You can't go on like this," Jake said one morning, as Shawna, dressed in a skirt and blouse, sipped a cup of coffee and scanned the newspaper without interest.

"Or *you* can't?" Shawna replied.

Jake's dog, Bruno, was lying under the table. With one brown eye and one blue, he stared at Maestro and growled as the precocious tabby hopped onto the window ledge. Crouching behind a broad-leafed plant, his tail twitching, Maestro glared longingly past the glass panes to the hanging bird-feeder where several snowbirds pecked at seeds.

Jake refused to be distracted. "If you don't believe that you're moping around here, take a look in the mirror, for Pete's sake."

"No, thank you."

"Shawna, you're killing yourself," Jake accused, sitting angrily in the chair directly across from hers.

"I'm leaving, just as soon as I find a place."

"I don't care about that, for crying out loud."

"I'm not 'moping' or 'killing myself' so don't you dare try to psychoanalyze me," she warned, raising her eyes to stare at him over the rim of her cup. He didn't have to remind her that she looked bad, for heaven's sake. She could *feel* it.

"Someone's got to," Jake grumbled. "You and Parker are so damned bullheaded."

Her heartbeat quickened at the sound of his name. If only he'd missed her!

"He looks twice as bad as you do."

"That's encouraging," she muttered, but hated the sound of her voice. Deep down, she wanted Parker to be happy and well.

"Talk to him."

"No."

"He's called twice."

Frowning, Shawna set her cup on the table. "It's over, Jake. That's the way he wanted it, and I'm tired of being treated as if my emotions don't mean a damned thing. Whether he meant to or not, he found my heart, threw it to the ground, and then stomped all over it."

"So now you don't care?"

"I didn't say that! And you're doing it again. Don't talk to me like you're my shrink, for Pete's sake."

Jake wouldn't be silenced. "Okay, so I'll talk like your brother. You're making one helluva mistake here."

"Not the first."

"Cut the bull, Shawna. I know you. You're hurting and you still love him even if you think he's a bastard. Isn't it worth just one more chance?"

She thought of the brass ring, still tucked secretly in the pocket of her robe. "Take a chance," Parker had told her at the fair that day. Dear Lord, it seemed ages ago.

"I'm out of chances."

Jake leaned over the table, his gaze fastened on her. "I've never thought you were stupid, Shawna. Don't change my mind, okay?" Glancing at the clock over the stove, he swore, grabbing his suit jacket from the back of a chair. "Do yourself a favor. Call him back." With this last bit of brotherly advice, Jake swung out the door, then returned, his face flushed. "And move your car, okay? Some of us have to work today."

She felt like sticking her tongue out at him, but instead she grabbed her purse and keys and swung her coat over her shoulders. The beginning of a plan had begun to form in her mind—and if Jake was right about Parker . . .

"You don't have to leave," Jake said as they walked down the frost-crusted path to the garage. "Just move that miserable little car of yours."

"I think I'd better get started."

"Doing what?" he asked. "You have the next couple of days off, don't you?"

She grabbed the handle of her car door and flashed him a secretive smile as she climbed inside, "Maybe you're right. Maybe I should do more than mope around here."

"What's that supposed to mean?" he asked suspiciously.

"I'm not sure. But I'll let you know." Waving with one hand, she rammed her car into gear and backed out of his driveway. With only the barest idea of what she was planning, she parked in front of the house and waited until Jake had roared out of sight.

Spurred into action, she hurried back inside Jake's house, called her friend Gerri, and threw some clothes into a bag.

Her heart was in her throat as she climbed back into her car. She could barely believe the plan that had formed in her mind. Ignoring the screaming protests in her mind, she drove through the fog, heading north until she slammed on the brakes at the street leading toward the Willamette River and Parker's house.

Her hands were damp. What if he wasn't home? Or worse yet, what if he had company? Perhaps Melinda? *Well, that would be too damned bad. Because it's now or never!*

Her muscles were so rigid they ached as she drove, her jaw firm with determination as Parker's huge house loomed to the side of the road. Without hesitation, she cranked the wheel, coasted along the long asphalt drive and parked near the brick path leading to the front door.

Then, with all the confidence she could gather, she marched up the path and rang the bell.

Twelve

Shawna held her breath as the door swung inward, and Parker, dressed in cords and a soft sweater, stared at her. Her heart started knocking against her ribcage as she looked into his eyes.

"Well, if this isn't a surprise," he drawled, not moving from the door. His face was unreadable. Not an emotion flickered in his eyes.

"I had a few things to sort out," she said.

"And are they sorted out?"

Nervously, she licked her lips. "Just about. I thought maybe we should talk, and I'm sorry I didn't return your calls."

Still suspicious, he pushed open the door. "Fair enough."

"Not here," she said quickly. "Someplace where we won't be disturbed."

"Such as?"

Shawna forced a friendly smile. "For starters, let's just drive."

He hesitated a minute, then shrugged, as if it didn't matter what she wanted to discuss—nothing would change. Yanking his fleece-lined jacket off the hall tree, he eyed his cane hanging on a hook but left it.

Striding back to the car, Shawna held her breath and felt his eyes bore into her back as he walked unsteadily after her and slid into the passenger side of the hatchback.

Without a word, she climbed behind the wheel and started out the drive. A surge of self-doubts assailed her. If he had any idea that she planned to kidnap him for the weekend, he'd be furious. She might have ruined any chance they had of ever getting back together again.

But it was a risk she had to take. The longer they were apart, she felt, the more likely stubborn pride would get in their way.

She put the little car through its paces, heading west amidst the fog still clinging to the upper reaches of the west hills. "So talk," Parker suggested, his arms crossed over his chest, his jean jacket stretched tight over his shoulders.

"I've had a lot of time to think," she said, gambling, not really knowing what to say now that he was sitting in the seat next to hers, his legs stretched close, his shoulder nearly touching hers. "And I think I acted rashly."

"We both behaved like children," he said, staring straight ahead as the city gave way to suburbs. Parker looked around, as if noticing for the first time that they'd left Portland far behind. Ahead the blue-gray mountains of the coast range loomed into view. "Where're we going?" he asked, suddenly apprehensive.

"To the beach." She didn't dare glance at him, afraid her emotions were mirrored in her eyes.

"The *beach*?" he repeated, stunned. "Why?"

"I think more clearly when I'm near the ocean." That, at least, wasn't a lie.

"But it's already afternoon. We won't be back until after dark."

"Is that a problem?"

"I guess not."

"Good. I know this great candy store in Cannon Beach—"

He groaned, and Shawna, glimpsing him from the corner of her eye, felt a growing sense of satisfaction. So he did remember—she could see it in his gaze. Earlier in the summer they'd visited Cannon Beach and eaten salt-water taffy until their stomachs ached. So just how much did he recall? Everything? What about Melinda? Shawna felt dread in her heart but steadfastly tamped it down. Tonight she'd face the truth—all of it. And so would Parker!

Once at the tiny coastal town, with its weathered buildings and cottages, they found a quaint restaurant high on the cliffs overlooking the sea. The beach was nearly deserted. Only a few hardy souls braved the sand and wind to stroll near the water's ragged edge. Gray-and-white sea gulls swooped from a steely sky, and rolling white-capped waves crashed against jagged black rocks as Shawna and Parker finished a meal of crab and crusty French bread.

"Want to take a walk?" Shawna asked.

Deep lines grooved around his mouth. "Didn't bring my wheelchair," he drawled, his lips thinning.

She said softly, "You can lean on me."

"I don't think so. I really should get back." His

eyes touched hers for a moment and then he glanced away, through the window and toward the sea.

"Melinda's expecting you?"

His jaw worked. "Actually, it's a case of my lawyer wants to meet with her attorney. That sort of thing."

She braced herself for the showdown. "Then we'd better get going," she said as if she had every intention of driving him back to Portland. "I wouldn't want to keep her waiting."

Parker paid the check, then ambled slowly toward the car. Shawna pointed across the street to a mom-and-pop grocery and deli. "I'll just be a minute. I want to pick up a few things," she said, jaywalking across the street.

"Can't you get whatever it is you need in Portland?"

Flashing him a mischievous smile, she shook her head. He noticed the luxuriant honey-blond waves that swept the back of her suede jacket. "Not fresh crab. Just give me a minute."

Rather than protest, he slid into the hatchback and Shawna joined him a few minutes later. She swallowed back her fear. Until this moment, she'd been fairly honest with him. But now, if she had the courage, she was going to lie through her teeth.

"It's almost sunset," she said, easing the car into the empty street.

The sun, a fiery luminous ball, was dropping slowly to the sea. The sky was tinged rosy hues of orange and lavender. "I'd noticed."

"Do you mind if I take the scenic route home, through Astoria?"

Frowning, Parker rubbed the back of his neck and shrugged. "I guess not. I'm late already."

So far, so good. She drove north along the rugged

coastline, following the curving road that wound along the crest of the cliffs overlooking the sea. Contorted pines and beach grass, gilded by the sun's final rays, flanked the asphalt. Parker closed his eyes and Shawna crossed her fingers. Maybe, just maybe, her plan would work.

"Here we are," Shawna said, pulling up the hand brake as the little car rolled to a stop.

Parker awakened slowly. He hadn't meant to doze, but he'd been exhausted for days. Ever since Shawna had moved out of his house, he'd spent sleepless nights in restless dreams filled with her, only to wake up drenched with sweat and hot with desire. His days, when he wasn't consulting his lawyer about Melinda's child, had been filled with physical therapy and swimming, and he could finally feel his body starting to respond. The pain in his injured leg had slowly lessened and his torn muscles had grudgingly started working again. For the first time since the accident, he'd felt a glimmer of hope that he would eventually walk unassisted again. That knowledge was his driving force, though it was a small comfort against the fact that he'd given up Shawna.

But only temporarily, he reminded himself, knowing that one way or another he would make her love him, not for what he once was, but for the man he'd become. But first, there was the matter of Melinda's baby, a matter which should have been completed this afternoon. If he'd had any brains at all, he never would have agreed to drive to the beach with Shawna, but he hadn't been able to stop himself.

When he had opened the door and found her,

smiling and radiant on his doorstep, he hadn't been able to resist spending a few hours with her.

Now, he blinked a couple of times, though he knew he wasn't dreaming. "Where?" In front of her car was a tiny, weathered run-down excuse of a cabin, behind which was the vibrantly sun-streaked ocean.

"Gerri's cabin."

"Gerri?"

"My friend. Remember?" She laughed a little nervously. "Come on, I bet you do. You seem to be remembering a lot lately. More than you're letting on."

But Parker still wasn't thinking straight. His gaze was glued to the gray shack with paned windows and a sagging porch. "What're we doing here?" Was he missing something?

She pocketed her keys, then faced him. "We're spending the weekend together. Here. Alone. No phone. No intrusions. Just you and me."

He smiled until he saw that she wasn't kidding. Her emerald eyes sparkled with determination. "Hey—wait a minute—"

But she wasn't listening. She climbed out of the car and grabbed the grocery bag.

"Shawna!" He wrenched open the door, watching in disbelief as she mounted the steps, searched with her fingers along the ledge over the porch, then, glancing back with a cat-who-ate-the-canary smile, held up a rusted key. *She wasn't joking!* "You can't do this—I've got to be back in Portland tonight!" Ignoring the pain in his knee, he followed after her, limping into the dark, musty interior of the cabin.

She was just lighting a kerosene lantern in the kitchen. "Romantic, don't you think?"

"What does romance have to do with the fact that you shanghaied me here?"

"Everything." She breezed past him and he couldn't help but notice the way her jeans fit snugly over her hips, or the scent of her hair, as she passed.

"I have a meeting—"

"It'll wait."

His blood was boiling. Just who the hell did she think she was—kidnapping him and then flirting with him so outrageously? If only she'd waited one more day! "Give me your keys," he demanded.

She laughed, a merry tinkling sound that bounced over the dusty rafters and echoed in the corners as she knelt on the hearth of a river-rock fireplace and opened the damper.

"I'm serious," Parker said.

"So am I. You're not getting the keys." She crumpled up a yellowed piece of newspaper, plunked two thick pieces of oak onto the grate, and lit a fire. Immediately flames crackled and leaped, climbing hungrily over the dry wood.

"Then I'll walk to the road and hitchhike."

"Guess again. It's nearly a mile. You're still recovering, remember?"

"Shawna—"

"Face it, Parker. This time, you're mine." Dusting her hands, she turned to face him and her expression had changed from playful and bright to sober. "And this time, I'm not letting you go. Not until we settle things once and for all."

Damn the woman! She had him and she knew it! And deep in his heart he was glad, even though he worried about his meeting with Melinda James and her attorney. He glanced around the room, past the sheet-draped furniture and rolled carpets to the windows and the view of the sea beyond. The sky was painted with lavender and magenta and the ocean, shimmering and restless, blazed gold. Worried that he might be blowing the delicate negotiations with Melinda, Parker shoved his hands into the pockets of his cords and waited. Protesting was getting him nowhere. "I'll have to make a call."

"Too bad."

He swore under his breath. "Who knows we're here?"

"Just Gerri. She owns this place."

Since Gerri was Shawna's best friend, he didn't doubt that she'd keep her mouth shut. "What about Jake or your folks?"

She shook her head and rolled out the carpet. "As I said, it's just you, me, the ocean, and the wind. And maybe, if you're lucky, white wine and grilled salmon."

"I'm afraid you'll live to regret this," he said, groaning inwardly as he deliberately advanced on her. Firelight caught in her hair and eyes, and a provocative dimple creased her cheek. The very essence of her seemed to fill the empty cracks and darkest corners of the cabin. He hadn't realized just how much he'd missed her until now. "We probably both will."

"I guess that's a chance we'll just have to take." She met his gaze then, her eyes filled with a love so pure, so intense, he felt guilty for not admitting that he remembered everything—that he, at this moment, had he been in Portland, would be planning for their future together. Reaching forward, he captured her wrist in his hand, felt her quivering pulse. "I want you to trust me," he said, his guts twisting when he recognized the pain in her eyes.

"I do," she whispered. "Why do you think I kidnapped you?"

"God only knows," he whispered, but his gaze centered on her softly parted lips and he felt a warm urgency invade his blood. "You know," he said, his voice turning silky, "I might just mete out my revenge for this little stunt."

He was close to her now, so close she could see the flecks of blue fire in his eyes. "Try me."

Would she never give up? He felt an incredible surge of pride that this gorgeous, intelligent woman loved him so tenaciously she would fight impossible odds to save their relationship. A vein throbbed in his temple, his thoughts filled with desire, and he gave in to the overpowering urge to forget about the past, the present, and the future as he gazed hungrily into her eyes. "I do love you. . . ." he whispered, sweeping her into his arms.

Shawna's heart soared, though she didn't have time to catch her breath. The kiss was hard, nearly brutal, and filled with a fierce passion that caused her heart to beat shamelessly.

She moaned in response, twining her arms around his neck, her breasts crushed against his chest, her blood hot with desire. He pulled her closer still, holding her so tight she could barely breathe as his tongue pressed against her teeth. Willingly her lips parted and she felt him explore the velvety recesses of her mouth.

"God, I've missed you," he whispered, his voice rough as his lips found her throat and moved slowly downward.

She didn't stop him when he pushed her jacket off her shoulders, nor did she protest when he undid the buttons of her blouse. Her eyes were bright when he kissed her lips again.

The fire glowed red and yellow and the sound of the sea crashing against rocks far below drifted through the open window as she helped him out of his clothes.

"Shawna—are you sure?" he asked, and groaned when she kissed his chest.

"I've always been sure," she whispered. "With you." Tasting the salt on his skin, feeling the ripple of his muscles, she breathed against him, wanton with pleasure when he sucked in his abdomen, his eyes glazing over.

"You're incredible," he murmured, moving suggestively against her, his arousal evident as her fingers played with his waistband, dipping lower and teasing him.

"So are you."

"If you don't stop me now—"

"Never," she replied and was rewarded with his wet lips pressing hard against hers. All control fled, and he pushed her to the carpet, his hands deftly removing her clothes and caressing her all over until she ached for more. Blood thundered in her ears, her heart slammed wildly in her chest, and she could only think of Parker and the desire throbbing hot in her veins. "I love you, Parker," she said, tears filling her eyes at the wonder of him.

Firelight gleamed on his skin as he lowered himself over her, touching the tip of her breasts with his tongue before taking one firm mound possessively with his mouth and suckling hungrily. His hand was on her back, spread wide over her skin, drawing her near as he rubbed against her, anxious and aroused.

"I should tell you—"

"Shh—" Twining her fingers in the hair of his nape, she drew his head down to hers and kissed him, moving her body erotically against his. She pushed his cords over his hips, her fingers inching down his muscular buttocks and thighs, a warm, primal need swirling deep within her. His clothes discarded, she ran her fingers over his skin and turned anxious lips to his.

If he wanted to stop, he couldn't. His muscles, glistening with sweat and reflecting the golden light from the fire, strained for one second before he parted her legs with one knee and thrust deep into her.

"Shawna," he cried, his hand on her breasts, his mouth raining kisses on her face. "Love me."

"I do!" Hot inside, and liquid, she captured him with her legs, arching against him and holding close, as if afraid he would disappear with the coming night.

With each of his long strokes, she felt as if she were on that carousel again, turning faster and faster, spinning wildly, crazily out of control.

Tangled in his passion, she shuddered, and the lights of the merry-go-round crackled and burst into brilliant blue and gold flames. Parker cried out, deeply and lustily, and it echoed with her own shriek of pleasure. Tears filled her eyes with each hot wave of pleasure that spread to her limbs.

Parker kissed the dewy perspiration from her forehead, then took an old blanket from the couch and wrapped it over them.

"My darling, I love you," he murmured, his voice cracking.

"You don't have to say anything," she whispered, but her heart fairly burst with love.

"Why lie?" Levering himself on one elbow, he brushed the honey-streaked strands of hair from her face and stared down at her. "You wouldn't believe me anyway. You've always insisted that I loved you." He kissed her gently on the cheek. "You just have no idea how much." His gaze lowered again, to the fullness of her breasts, the pinch of her waist, the length of her legs. "I love you more than any sane man should love a woman," he admitted, his voice thick with emotion.

"Now, we can forget about everything except each other," she whispered, winding her arms around his neck. "I love you, Parker Harrison. And I want you. And if all I can have of you is this one weekend— then I'll take it."

"Not good enough, Doctor," he said, his smile white and sensual as it slashed across his jaw. "With you, it has to be forever."

"Forever it is," she whispered, her voice breaking as she tilted her face eagerly to his.

Gathering her into his arms, he made love to her all night long.

Thirteen

Shawna stretched lazily on the bed, smiling to herself as she reached for Parker again. But her fingers rubbed only cold sheets. Her eyes flew open. "Parker?" she called, glancing around the tiny bedroom. Where was he?

Morning light streamed into the room and the old lace curtains fluttered in the breeze.

"Parker?" she called again, rubbing her eyes before scrambling for her robe. The little cabin was cold and she didn't hear any sounds of life from the other room. There was a chance he'd hobbled down to the beach, but she doubted he would climb down the steep stairs of the cliff face. Worried, she crossed the small living room to peer out a side window, and her fears were confirmed. Her hatchback was gone. He'd left. After a night of intense lovemaking, he'd gone.

Maybe he's just gone to the store, or to find a phone booth, she told herself, but she knew better, even before she found a hastily scrawled note on the table. Her hands shook as she picked up a small scrap of paper and read:

> Had to run home for a while. I'll be back or send someone for you. Trust me. I do love you.

She crumpled the note in her hand and shoved it into the pocket of her robe. Her fingers grazed the cold metal of the brass ring he'd won at the fair all those weeks ago and she dropped into one of the old, dilapidated chairs. Why had he returned to Portland?

To settle things with Melinda.

And after that?

Who knows?

Her head fell to her hands, but she tried to think positively. He did love her. He had admitted it over and over again the night before while making love, and again in the note. So why leave? Why take off and abandon her now?

"Serves you right," she muttered, thinking how she'd shanghaied him to this cabin.

She had two options: she could walk into town and call her brother, or trust Parker and wait it out. This time, she decided to give Parker the benefit of the doubt.

To pass the time, she cleaned the house, stacked wood, even started lamb stew simmering on the stove before changing into clean clothes. But at five-thirty, when he hadn't shown up again, she couldn't buoy her deflated spirits. The longer he was away, the more uncertain she was of the words of love he had whispered in the night.

"He'll be back," she told herself, knowing he wouldn't leave her stranded, not even to pay her back for tricking him. Nonetheless, she slipped into her shoes and jacket and walked outside.

The air was cool and as the sun set, fog collected over the waves. A salty breeze caught and tangled in her hair as she threaded her way along an over-grown path to the stairs. Brambles and skeletal berry vines clung to her clothes and dry beach grass rubbed against her jeans before she reached the weathered steps that zigzagged back and forth along the cliff face and eventually led to the beach. She hurried down, her shoes catching on the uneven boards and exposed nails, to the deserted crescent-shaped strip of white sand. Sea gulls cried over the roar of the surf and foamy waves crashed against barnacle-riddled shoals. Far to the north a solitary lighthouse knifed upward, no light shining from its gleaming white tower.

Shawna stuffed her hands in her pockets and walked along the water's edge, eyeing the lavender sky and a few stars winking through tattered wisps of fog. She walked aimlessly, her thoughts as turbu-lent as the restless waves.

Why hadn't Parker returned? Why? Why? Why?

She kicked at an agate and turned back toward the stairs, her eyes following the ridge. Then she saw him, standing at the top of the cliff, balanced on the weather-beaten stairs. His hair ruffling in the wind, Parker was staring down at her.

He'd come back!

Her heart took flight and she started running along the water's edge. All her doubts were washed away with the tide. He waved, then started down the stairs.

"Parker, no! Wait!" she called, her breath short. The steps were uneven, and because of his leg, she was afraid he might fall. Fear curled over her heart as she saw him stumble and catch himself. "Parker— don't—"

But her words were caught in the wind and drowned by the roar of the sea. Adrenaline spurred her on, her gaze fastened on the stairs. He was slowly inching his way down, his hands gripping the rail, but she was still worried.

Her legs felt like lead as she raced across the dry sand toward the stairs, her heart hammering, slamming against her ribs, as his eyes locked with hers. He grinned and stepped down, only to miss the final sun-bleached stairs.

"No!" she cried, as he scrambled against the rail, swore, then pitched forward. In an awful instant, she watched as he fell onto the sand, his strong outstretched arms breaking his fall. But his jeans caught on a nail, the fabric ripped, and his bad leg wrenched.

He cried out as he landed on the sand.

"Parker!" Shawna flew to his side, dropping to her knees in the sand, touching his face, her hands tracing the familiar line of his jaw as his eyes blinked open.

"You—you were supposed to catch me," he joked, but the lines near his mouth were white with pain.

"And you weren't supposed to fall! Are you all right?" She cradled his head to her breast, her eyes glancing down to his leg.

"Better now," he admitted, still grimacing a little, but his blue gaze tangled in hers.

"Let me see—"

Ignoring his protests, she ripped his pant leg further and probed gently at his knee.

He inhaled swiftly.

"Well, you didn't do it any good, but you'll live," she thought aloud, relieved that nothing seemed to have torn. "But you'll have to have it looked at when we get back." She tossed her hair over her shoulder and glared at him. "That was a stupid move, Harrison—" she said, noticing for the first time a crisp white envelope in the sand. "What's this?"

"The adoption papers," he replied, stretching his leg and grimacing.

"Adoption—?" Her eyes flew to his.

"Melinda's agreed to let me adopt the baby."

"You—?"

"Yep." Forcing himself to a standing position, he steadied himself on the rail as Shawna scanned the legal forms. "It didn't even take much convincing. I agreed to send her to school and take care of the baby. That's all she really wanted."

Shawna eyed him suspiciously and dusted off her hands to stand next to him. "Are you sure you're okay?"

His eyes darkened with the night. "I'm fine, now that everything's worked out. You know the baby isn't really mine. Melinda was Brad's girlfriend. I just couldn't remember the connection for a while."

She couldn't believe her ears. "What triggered your memory?"

"You did," he said affectionately. "You literally jarred me to my senses when you moved out."

Dumbstruck, she felt her mouth open and close—then her eyes glimmered furiously. "That was days ago!"

"I called."

Trying to hold onto her indignation, she placed her hands on her hips. "You could have said something last night!"

"I was busy last night," he said and her heart began to pound. "So, do you want to know what happened?"

"Of course."

"The night of the wedding rehearsal, I drove Brad to Melinda's apartment and they had a knock-down-drag-out about her pregnancy. He didn't want to be tied down to a wife and kid—thought it would interfere with his career." Parker whitened at the memory. "Melinda was so upset she slapped him and he passed out on the couch. That's why I remembered her, because I held her, told her everything would work out, and tried to talk some sense into her. Later, I intended to give Brad the lecture of his life. But," he sighed, "I didn't get the chance."

"So why did she claim the baby was yours?"

"Because she blamed me for Brad's death. It was a scheme she and her father cooked up when they read in the papers that I had amnesia. But she couldn't go through with it."

"Because you remembered."

"No, because she finally realized she had to do what was best for the baby. Nothing else mattered."

"That's a little hard to believe," Shawna whispered.

He shrugged. "I guess the maternal instinct is stronger than either of us suspected. Anyway, I told her I'd help her through school, but I want full custody of the child." His eyes narrowed on the sea and now, as if to shake off the past, he struggled to stand. "It's the least I can do for Brad."

"Be careful," she instructed as she brushed the sand from her jeans. She, too, was reeling. Parker was going to be a father!

Wincing a little, he tried his leg, then slung his arm over Shawna's shoulders. "I guess I'll just have to lean on you," he whispered, "if you'll let me."

"You think I wouldn't?"

Shrugging he squeezed her shoulder. "I've been kind of an ass," he admitted.

"That's for sure," she agreed, but she grinned up at him as they walked toward the ocean. "But I can handle you."

"Can you? How about a baby?"

She stopped dead in her tracks. "What are you saying, Parker?" They were at the water's edge, the tide lapping around her feet.

"I'm asking you to marry me, Shawna," he whispered, his gaze delving deep into hers. "I'm asking you to help me raise Brad's baby, as if it were ours, and I'm begging you to love me for who I am, not the man I was," he said, stripping his soul bare, his eyes dark with conviction.

"But I do—"

"I'm not the same man you planned to marry before," he pointed out, giving her one last door to walk through, though his fingers tightened possessively around her shoulders.

"Of course you are. Don't you know that no matter what happens in our lives, what tragedy strikes, I'll never leave you—and not just out of some sense of duty," she explained, "but because I love you."

She saw the tears gather in his eyes, noticed the quivering of his chin. "You're sure about this?"

"I haven't been chasing you down for weeks, bulldozing my way into your life just because I thought it was the right thing to do, Parker."

"I know, but—"

" 'I know but' nothing. I love *you*—not some gilded memory!"

"All this time I thought—"

"That's the problem, Parker, you didn't think," she said, poking a finger into his broad chest and grinning.

"Oh how I love you," he said, his arms pulling her swiftly to him, his lips crashing down on hers, his hands twining in the long silky strands of her hair.

The kiss was filled with the wonder and promise of the future and her heart began to beat a wild cadence. "I'll never let you go now," he vowed.

"I don't want to."

"But if you ever decide to leave me," he warned, his eyes drilling into hers. "I'll hunt you down, Shawna, I swear it. And I'll make you love me again."

"You won't have to." She heard the driving beat of his heart over the thrashing sea, saw pulsating desire in his blue eyes, and melted against him. "I'll never leave." She tasted salt from his tears as she kissed him again.

"Good. Then maybe we can exchange this—" Reaching into his pocket, he withdrew the beribboned brass ring.

"Where did you get that?"

"In the cabin, where you were supposed to be."

"But what're you going to do?"

"We don't need this any more." Grinning wickedly, he hurled the ring with its fluttering ribbons out to sea.

"Parker, no!" she cried.

But the ring was airborne, flying into the dusk before settling into the purple water.

"As I was saying, we'll exchange the brass ring for two gold bands."

She watched as pastel ribbons drifted beneath the foaming waves. When he tilted her face upward, her eyes were glistening with tears. Finally, Parker had come home. Nothing separated them.

"Will you marry me, Dr. McGuire?"

"Yes," she whispered, her voice catching as she flung her arms around his neck and pressed her eager lips to his. He loved her and he remembered! Finally, they would be together! "Yes, oh, yes!" Her green eyes shimmered in the deepening shadows, her hands urgent as desire and happiness swept through her.

"Slow down, Shawna," he whispered roughly. But even as he spoke, her weight was dragging them both down to the sea-kissed sand. "We've got the rest of our lives."

THE EDITOR'S CORNER

What a wonderful summer of romance reading we have in store for you. Truly, you're going to be LOVESWEPT with some happy surprises through the long, hot, lazy days ahead.

First, you're going to get **POCKETS FULL OF JOY**, LOVESWEPT #270, by our new Canadian author, Judy Gill. Elaina McIvor wondered helplessly what she was going to do with an eleven-month-old baby to care for. Dr. "Brad" Bradshaw had been the stork and deposited the infant on her doorstep and raced away. But he was back soon enough to "play doctor" and "play house" in one of the most delightful and sensuous romances of the season.

Joan Elliott Pickart has created two of her most intriguing characters ever in **TATTERED WINGS**, LOVESWEPT #271. Devastatingly handsome Mark Hampton—an Air Force Colonel whose once exciting life now seems terribly lonely—and beautiful, enigmatic Eden Landry—a top fashion model who left her glamorous life for a secluded ranch—meet one snowy night. Desire flares immediately. But so do problems. Mark soon discovers that Eden is like a perfect butterfly encased in a cube of glass. You'll revel in the ways he finds to break down the walls without hurting the woman!

For all of you who've written to ask for Tara's and Jed's love story, here your fervent requests

(continued)

are answered with Barbara Boswell's terrific **AND TARA, TOO,** LOVESWEPT #272. As we know, Jed Ramsey is as darkly sleek and as seductive and as winning with women as a man can be. And Tara Brady wants no part of him. It would be just too convenient, she thinks, if all the Brady sisters married Ramsey men. But that's exactly what Jed's tyrannical father has in mind. You'll chuckle and gasp as Tara and Jed rattle the chains of fate in a breathlessly sensual and touching love story.

Margie McDonnell is an author who can transport you to another world. This time she takes you to **THE LAND OF ENCHANTMENT,** via LOVESWEPT #273, to meet a modern-day, ever so gallant knight, dashing Patrick Knight, and the sensitive and lovely Karen Harris. Karen is the single parent of an exceptional son and a quite sensible lady . . . until she falls for the handsome hunk who is as merry as he is creative. We think you'll delight in this very special, very thrilling love story.

It gives us enormous pleasure next month to celebrate the fifth anniversary of Iris Johansen's writing career. Her first ever published book was LOVESWEPT's **STORMY VOWS** in August 1983. With that and its companion romance **TEMPEST AT SEA,** published in September 1983, Iris launched the romance featuring spin-off and/or continuing characters. Now everyone's doing it! But, still,

(continued)

nobody does it quite like the woman who began it all, Iris Johansen. Here, next month, you'll meet old friends and new lovers in **BLUE SKIES AND SHINING PROMISES,** LOVESWEPT #274. (The following month she'll also have a LOVESWEPT, of course, and we wonder if you can guess who the featured characters will be.) Don't miss the thrilling love story of Cameron Bandor (yes, you know him) and Damita Shaughnessy, whose background will shock, surprise and move you, taking you right back to five years ago!

Welcome, back, Peggy Webb! In the utterly bewitching LOVESWEPT #275, **SLEEPLESS NIGHTS,** Peggy tells the story of Tanner Donovan of the quicksilver eyes and Amanda Lassiter of the tart tongue and tender heart. In this thrilling and sensuous story, you have a marvelous battle of wits between lovers parted in the past and determined to best each other in the present. A real delight!

As always, we hope that not one of our LOVE-SWEPTs will ever disappoint you. Enjoy!

Carolyn Nichols

Carolyn Nichols
  Editor
LOVESWEPT
Bantam Books
666 Fifth Avenue
New York, NY 10103

THE HOMETOWN HUNK CONTEST

FOR EVERY WOMAN WHO HAS EVER SAID—
"I know a man who looks
just like the hero of this book"
—HAVE WE GOT A CONTEST FOR YOU!

To help celebrate our fifth year of publishing LOVESWEPT we are having a fabulous, fun-filled event called THE HOMETOWN HUNK contest. We are going to reissue six classic early titles by six of your favorite authors.

DARLING OBSTACLES by Barbara Boswell
IN A CLASS BY ITSELF by Sandra Brown
C.J.'S FATE by Kay Hooper
THE LADY AND THE UNICORN by Iris Johansen
CHARADE by Joan Elliott Pickart
FOR THE LOVE OF SAMI by Fayrene Preston

Here, as in the backs of all July, August, and September 1988 LOVESWEPTS you will find "cover notes" just like the ones we prepare at Bantam as the background for our art director to create our covers. These notes will describe the hero and heroine, give a teaser on the plot, and suggest a scene for the cover. Your part in the contest will be to see if a great looking local man—or men, if your hometown is so blessed—fits our description of one of the heroes of the six books we will reissue.

THE HOMETOWN HUNK who is selected (one for each of the six titles) will be flown to New York via United Airlines and will stay at the Loews Summit Hotel—the ideal hotel for business or pleasure in midtown Manhattan—for two nights. All travel arrangements made by Reliable Travel International, Incorporated. He will be the model for the new cover of the book which will be released in mid-1989. The six people who send in the winning photos of their HOMETOWN HUNK will receive a pre-selected assortment of LOVESWEPT books free for one year. Please see the Official Rules above the Official Entry Form for full details and restrictions.

We can't wait to start judging those pictures! Oh, and you must let the man you've chosen know that you're entering him in the contest. After all, if he wins he'll have to come to New York.

Have fun. Here's your chance to get the cover-lover of your dreams!

Carolyn Nichols

Carolyn Nichols
Editor
LOVESWEPT
Bantam Books
666 Fifth Avenue
New York, NY 10102–0023

THE HOMETOWN HUNK CONTEST

DARLING OBSTACLES
(Originally Published as LOVESWEPT #95)
By Barbara Boswell

COVER NOTES

The Characters:

Hero:
GREG WILDER's gorgeous body and "to-die-for" good looks haven't hurt him in the dating department, but when most women discover he's a widower with four kids, they head for the hills! Greg has the hard, muscular build of an athlete, and his light brown hair, which he wears neatly parted on the side, is streaked blond by the sun. Add to that his aquamarine blue eyes that sparkle when he laughs, and his sensual mouth and generous lower lip, and you're probably wondering what woman in her right mind wouldn't want Greg's strong, capable surgeon's hands working their magic on her—kids or no kids!

Personality Traits:
An acclaimed neurosurgeon, Greg Wilder is a celebrity of sorts in the planned community of Woodland, Maryland. Authoritative, debonair, self-confident, his reputation for engaging in one casual relationship after another almost overshadows his prowess as a doctor. In reality, Greg dates more out of necessity than anything else, since he has to attend one social function after another. He considers most of the events boring and wishes he could spend more time with his children. But his profession is a difficult and demanding one—and being both father and mother to four kids isn't any less so. A thoughtful, generous, sometimes befuddled father, Greg tries to do it all. Cerebral, he uses his intellect and skill rather than physical strength to win his victories. However, he never expected to come up against one Mary Magdalene May!

Heroine:
MARY MAGDALENE MAY, called Maggie by her friends, is the thirty-two-year-old mother of three children. She has shoulder-length auburn hair, and green eyes that shout her Irish heritage. With high cheekbones and an upturned nose covered with a smattering of freckles, Maggie thinks of herself more as the girl-next-door type. Certainly, she believes, she could never be one of Greg Wilder's beautiful escorts.

Setting: The small town of Woodland, Maryland

The Story:
Surgeon Greg Wilder wanted to court the feisty and beautiful widow who'd been caring for his four kids, but she just wouldn't let him past her doorstep! Sure that his interest was only casual, and that he preferred more sophisticated women, Maggie May vowed to keep Greg at arm's length. But he wouldn't take no for an answer. And once he'd crashed through her defenses and pulled her into his arms, he was tireless—and reckless—in his campaign to win her over. Maggie had found it tough enough to resist one determined doctor; now he threatened to call in his kids and hers as reinforcements—seven rowdy snags to romance!

Cover scene:
As if romancing Maggie weren't hard enough, Greg can't seem to find time to spend with her without their children around. Stealing a private moment on the stairs in Maggie's house, Greg and Maggie embrace. She is standing one step above him, but she still has to look up at him to see into his eyes. Greg's hands are on her hips, and her hands are resting on his shoulders. Maggie is wearing a very sheer, short pink nightgown, and Greg has on wheat-colored jeans and a navy and yellow striped rugby shirt. Do they have time to kiss?

THE HOMETOWN HUNK CONTEST

IN A CLASS BY ITSELF
(Originally Published as LOVESWEPT #66)
By Sandra Brown

COVER NOTES

The Characters:

Hero:
LOGAN WEBSTER would have no trouble posing for a
Scandinavian travel poster. His wheat-colored hair always
seems to be tousled, defying attempts to control it, and
falls across his wide forehead. Thick eyebrows one shade
darker than his hair accentuate his crystal blue eyes. He
has a slender nose that flairs slightly over a mouth that
testifies to both sensitivity and strength. The faint lines
around his eyes and alongside his mouth give the impression that reaching the ripe age of 30 wasn't all fun and
games for him. Logan's square, determined jaw is punctu-
ated by a vertical cleft. His broad shoulders and narrow
waist add to his tall, lean appearance.

Personality traits:
Logan Webster has had to scrape and save and fight for
everything he's gotten. Born into a poor farm family, he
was driven to succeed and overcome his "wrong side of
the tracks" image. His businesses include cattle, real estate, and natural gas. Now a pillar of the community,
Logan's life has been a true rags-to-riches story. Only
Sandra Brown's own words can describe why he is masculinity epitomized: "Logan had 'the walk,' that saddle-
tramp saunter that was inherent to native Texan men,
passed down through generations of cowboys. It was, without even trying to be, sexy. The unconscious roll of the
hips, the slow strut, the flexed knees, the slouching stance,
the deceptive laziness that hid a latent aggressiveness."
Wow! And not only does he have "the walk," but he's fun

and generous and kind. Even with his wealth, he feels at home living in his small hometown with simple, hard-working, middle-class, backbone-of-America folks. A born leader, people automatically gravitate toward him.

Heroine:
DANI QUINN is a sophisticated twenty-eight-year-old woman. Dainty, her body compact, she is utterly feminine. Dani's pale, lustrous hair is moonlight and honey spun together, and because it is very straight, she usually wears it in a chignon. With golden eyes to match her golden hair, Dani is the one woman Logan hasn't been able to get off his mind for the ten years they've been apart.

Setting: Primarily on Logan's ranch in East Texas.

The Story:
Ten years had passed since Dani Quinn had graduated from high school in the small Texas town, ten years since the night her elopement with Logan Webster had ended in disaster. Now Dani approached her tenth reunion with uncertainty. Logan would be there . . . Logan, the only man who'd ever made her shiver with desire and need, but would she have the courage to face the fury in his eyes? She couldn't defend herself against his anger and hurt—to do so would demand she reveal the secret sorrow she shared with no one. Logan's touch had made her his so long ago. Could he reach past the pain to make her his for all time?

Cover Scene:
It's sunset, and Logan and Dani are standing beside the swimming pool on his ranch, embracing. The pool is surrounded by semitropical plants and lush flower beds. In the distance, acres of rolling pasture land resembling a green lake undulate into dense, piney woods. Dani is wearing a strapless, peacock blue bikini and sandals with leather ties that wrap around her ankles. Her hair is straight and loose, falling to the middle of her back. Logan has on a light-colored pair of corduroy shorts and a short-sleeved designer knit shirt in a pale shade of yellow.

THE HOMETOWN HUNK CONTEST

C.J.'S FATE
(Originally Published as LOVESWEPT #32)
By Kay Hooper

COVER NOTES

The Characters:

Hero:
FATE WESTON easily could have walked straight off an Indian reservation. His raven black hair and strong, well-molded features testify to his heritage. But somewhere along the line genetics threw Fate a curve—his eyes are the deepest, darkest blue imaginable! Above those blue eyes are dark slanted eyebrows, and fanning out from those eyes are faint laugh lines—the only sign of the fact that he's thirty-four years old. Tall, Fate moves with easy, loose-limbed grace. Although he isn't an athlete, Fate takes very good care of himself, and it shows in his strong physique. Striking at first glance and fascinating with each succeeding glance, the serious expressions on his face make him look older than his years, but with one smile he looks boyish again.

Personality traits:
Fate possesses a keen sense of humor. His heavy-lidded, intelligent eyes are capable of concealment, but there is a shrewdness in them that reveals the man hadn't needed college or a law degree to be considered intelligent. The set of his head tells you that he is proud—perhaps even a bit arrogant. He is attractive and perfectly well aware of that fact. Unconventional, paradoxical, tender, silly, lusty, gentle, comical, serious, absurd, and endearing are all words that come to mind when you think of Fate. He is not ashamed to be everything a man can be. A defense attorney by profession, one can detect a bit of frustrated actor in his character. More than anything else, though, it's the

impression of humor about him—reinforced by the elusive dimple in his cheek—that makes Fate Weston a scrumptious hero!

Heroine:
C.J. ADAMS is a twenty-six-year-old research librarian. Unaware of her own attractiveness, C.J. tends to play down her pixylike figure and tawny gold eyes. But once she meets Fate, she no longer feels that her short, burnished copper curls and the sprinkling of freckles on her nose make her unappealing. He brings out the vixen in her, and changes the smart, bookish woman who professed to have no interest in men into the beautiful, sexy woman she really was all along. Now, if only he could get her to tell him what C.J. stands for!

Setting: Ski lodge in Aspen, Colorado

The Story:
C.J. Adams had been teased enough about her seeming lack of interest in the opposite sex. On a ski trip with her five best friends, she impulsively embraced a handsome stranger, pretending they were secret lovers—and the delighted lawyer who joined in her impetuous charade seized the moment to deepen the kiss. Astonished at his reaction, C.J. tried to nip their romance in the bud—but found herself nipping at his neck instead! She had met her match in a man who could answer her witty remarks with clever ripostes of his own, and a lover whose caresses aroused in her a passionate need she'd never suspected that she could feel. Had destiny somehow tossed them together?

Cover Scene:
C.J. and Fate virtually have the ski slopes to themselves early one morning, and they take advantage of it! Frolicking in a snow drift, Fate is covering C.J. with snow—and kisses! They are flushed from the cold weather and from the excitement of being in love. C.J. is wearing a sky-blue, one-piece, tight-fitting ski outfit that zips down the front. Fate is wearing a navy blue parka and matching ski pants.

THE HOMETOWN HUNK CONTEST

THE LADY AND THE UNICORN
(Originally Published as LOVESWEPT #29)
By Iris Johansen

COVER NOTES

The Characters:

Hero:
Not classically handsome, RAFE SANTINE's blunt, craggy
features reinforce the quality of overpowering virility about
him. He has wide, Slavic cheekbones and a bold, thrust-
ing chin, which give the impression of strength and authority. Thick black eyebrows are set over piercing dark
eyes. He wears his heavy, dark hair long. His large frame
measures in at almost six feet four inches, and it's hard to
believe that a man with such brawny shoulders and strong
thighs could exhibit the pantherlike grace which charac-
terizes Rafe's movements. Rafe Santine is definitely a man
to be reckoned with, and heroine Janna Cannon does just
that!

Personality traits:
Our hero is a man who radiates an aura of power and
danger, and women find him intriguing and irresistible.
Rafe Santine is a self-made billionaire at the age of thirty-
eight. Almost entirely self-educated, he left school at six-
teen to work on his first construction job, and by the time
he was twenty-three, he owned the company. From there
he branched out into real estate, computers, and oil. Rafe
reportedly changes mistresses as often as he changes shirts.
His reputation for ruthless brilliance has been earned over
years of fighting to the top of the economic ladder from
the slums of New York. His gruff manner and hard personality hide the tender, vulnerable side of him. Rafe also
possesses an insatiable thirst for knowledge that is a
passion with him. Oddly enough, he has a wry sense of

humor that surfaces unexpectedly from time to time. And, though cynical to the extreme, he never lets his natural skepticism interfere with his innate sense of justice.

Heroine:
JANNA CANNON, a game warden for a small wildlife preserve, is a very dedicated lady. She is tall at five feet nine inches and carries herself in a stately way. Her long hair is dark brown and is usually twisted into a single thick braid in back. Of course, Rafe never lets her keep her hair braided when they make love! Janna is one quarter Cherokee Indian by heritage, and she possesses the dark eyes and skin of her ancestors.

Setting: Rafe's estate in Carmel, California

The Story:
Janna Cannon scaled the high walls of Rafe Santine's private estate, afraid of nothing and determined to appeal to the powerful man who could save her beloved animal preserve. She bewitched his guard dogs, then cast a spell of enchantment over him as well. Janna's profound grace, her caring nature, made the tough and proud Rafe grow mercurial in her presence. She offered him a gift he'd never risked reaching out for before—but could he trust his own emotions enough to open himself to her love?

Cover Scene:
In the gazebo overlooking the rugged cliffs at the edge of the Pacific Ocean, Rafe and Janna share a passionate moment together. The gazebo is made of redwood and the interior is small and cozy. Scarlet cushions cover the benches, and matching scarlet curtains hang from the eaves, caught back by tasseled sashes to permit the sea breeze to whip through the enclosure. Rafe is wearing black suede pants and a charcoal gray crew-neck sweater. Janna is wearing a safari-style khaki shirt-and-slacks outfit and suede desert boots. They embrace against the breathtaking backdrop of wild, crashing, white-crested waves pounding the rocks and cliffs below.

THE HOMETOWN HUNK CONTEST

CHARADE
(Originally Published as LOVESWEPT #74)
By Joan Elliott Pickart

COVER NOTES

The Characters:

Hero:
The phrase tall, dark, and handsome was coined to describe TENNES WHITNEY. His coal black hair reaches past his collar in back, and his fathomless steel gray eyes are framed by the kind of thick, dark lashes that a woman would kill to have. Darkly tanned, Tennes has a straight nose and a square chin, with—you guessed it!—a Kirk Douglas cleft. Tennes oozes masculinity and virility. He's a handsome son-of-a-gun!

Personality traits:
A shrewd, ruthless business tycoon, Tennes is a man of strength and principle. He's perfected the art of buying floundering companies and turning them around financially, then selling them at a profit. He possesses a sixth sense about business—in short, he's a winner! But there are two sides to his personality. Always in cool command, Tennes, who fears no man or challenge, is rendered emotionally vulnerable when faced with his elderly aunt's illness. His deep devotion to the woman who raised him clearly casts him as a warm, compassionate guy—not at all like the tough-as-nails executive image he presents. Leave it to heroine Whitney Jordan to discover the real man behind the complicated enigma.

Heroine:
WHITNEY JORDAN's russet-colored hair floats past her shoulders in glorious waves. Her emerald green eyes, full breasts, and long, slender legs—not to mention her peaches-

and-cream complexion—make her eye-poppingly attractive. How can Tennes resist the twenty-six-year-old beauty? And how can Whitney consider becoming serious with him? If their romance flourishes, she may end up being Whitney Whitney!

Setting: Los Angeles, California

The Story:
One moment writer Whitney Jordan was strolling the aisles of McNeil's Department Store, plotting the untimely demise of a soap opera heartthrob; the next, she was nearly knocked over by a real-life stunner who implored her to be his fiancée! The ailing little gray-haired aunt who'd raised him had one final wish, he said—to see her dear nephew Tennes married to the wonderful girl he'd described in his letters . . . only that girl hadn't existed—until now! Tennes promised the masquerade would last only through lunch, but Whitney gave such an inspired performance that Aunt Olive refused to let her go. And what began as a playful romantic deception grew more breathlessly real by the minute. . . .

Cover Scene:
Whitney's living room is bright and cheerful. The gray carpeting and blue sofa with green and blue throw pillows gives the apartment a cool but welcoming appearance. Sitting on the sofa next to Tennes, Whitney is wearing a black crepe dress that is simply cut but stunning. It is cut low over her breasts and held at the shoulders by thin straps. The skirt falls to her knees in soft folds and the bodice is nipped in at the waist with a matching belt. She has on black high heels, but prefers not to wear any jewelry to spoil the simplicity of the dress. Tennes is dressed in a black suit with a white silk shirt and a deep red tie.

THE HOMETOWN HUNK CONTEST

FOR THE LOVE OF SAMI
(Originally Published as LOVESWEPT #34)
By Fayrene Preston

COVER NOTES

Hero:
DANIEL PARKER-ST. JAMES is every woman's dream come true. With glossy black hair and warm, reassuring blue eyes, he makes our heroine melt with just a glance. Daniel's lean face is chiseled into assertive planes. His lips are full and firmly sculptured, and his chin has the determined and arrogant thrust to it only a man who's sure of himself can carry off. Daniel has a lot in common with Clark Kent. Both wear glasses, and when Daniel removes them to make love to Sami, she thinks he really is Superman!

Personality traits:
Daniel Parker-St. James is one of the Twin Cities' most respected attorneys. He's always in the news, either in the society columns with his latest society lady, or on the front page with his headline cases. He's brilliant and takes on only the toughest cases—usually those that involve millions of dollars. Daniel has a reputation for being a deadly opponent in the courtroom. Because he's from a socially prominent family and is a Harvard graduate, it's expected that he'll run for the Senate one day. Distinguished-looking and always distinctively dressed—he's fastidious about his appearance—Daniel gives off an unassailable air of authority and absolute control.

Heroine:
SAMUELINA (SAMI) ADKINSON is secretly a wealthy heiress. No one would guess. She lives in a converted warehouse loft, dresses to suit no one but herself, and dabbles in the creative arts. Sami is twenty-six years old, with

long, honey-colored hair. She wears soft, wispy bangs and has very thick brown lashes framing her golden eyes. Of medium height, Sami has to look up to gaze into Daniel's deep blue eyes.

Setting: St. Paul, Minnesota

The Story:
Unpredictable heiress Sami Adkinson had endeared herself to the most surprising people—from the bag ladies in the park she protected . . . to the mobster who appointed himself her guardian . . . to her exasperated but loving friends. Then Sami was arrested while demonstrating to save baby seals, and it took powerful attorney Daniel Parker-St. James to bail her out. Daniel was smitten, soon cherishing Sami and protecting her from her night fears. Sami reveled in his love—and resisted it too. And holding on to Sami, Daniel discovered, was like trying to hug quicksilver. . . .

Cover Scene:
The interior of Daniel's house is very grand and supremely formal, the decor sophisticated, refined, and quietly tasteful, just like Daniel himself. Rich traditional fabrics cover plush oversized custom sofas and Regency wing chairs. Queen Anne furniture is mixed with Chippendale and is subtly complemented with Oriental accent pieces. In the library, floor-to-ceiling bookcases filled with rare books provide the backdrop for Sami and Daniel's embrace. Sami is wearing a gold satin sheath gown. The dress has a high neckline, but in back is cut provocatively to the waist. Her jewels are exquisite. The necklace is made up of clusters of flowers created by large, flawless diamonds. From every cluster a huge, perfectly matched teardrop emerald hangs. The earrings are composed of an even larger flower cluster, and an equally huge teardrop-shaped emerald hangs from each one. Daniel is wearing a classic, elegant tuxedo.

LOVESWEPT® HOMETOWN HUNK CONTEST

OFFICIAL RULES

> IN A CLASS BY ITSELF by Sandra Brown
> FOR THE LOVE OF SAMI by Fayrene Preston
> C.J.'S FATE by Kay Hooper
> THE LADY AND THE UNICORN by Iris Johansen
> CHARADE by Joan Elliott Pickart
> DARLING OBSTACLES by Barbara Boswell

1. NO PURCHASE NECESSARY. Enter the HOMETOWN HUNK contest by completing the Official Entry Form below and enclosing a sharp color full-length photograph (easy to see details, with the photo being no smaller than 2½" × 3½") of the man you think perfectly represents one of the heroes from the above-listed books which are described in the accompanying Loveswept cover notes. Please be sure to fill out the Official Entry Form completely, and also be sure to clearly print on the back of the man's photograph the man's name, address, city, state, zip code, telephone number, date of birth, your name, address, city, state, zip code, telephone number, your relationship, if any, to the man (e.g. wife, girlfriend) as well as the title of the Loveswept book for which you are entering the man. If you do not have an Official Entry Form, you can print all of the required information on a 3" × 5" card and attach it to the photograph with all the necessary information printed on the back of the photograph as well. YOUR HERO MUST SIGN BOTH THE BACK OF THE OFFICIAL ENTRY FORM (OR 3" × 5" CARD) AND THE PHOTOGRAPH TO SIGNIFY HIS CONSENT TO BEING ENTERED IN THE CONTEST. Completed entries should be sent to:

> BANTAM BOOKS
> HOMETOWN HUNK CONTEST
> Department CN
> 666 Fifth Avenue
> New York, New York 10102–0023

All photographs and entries become the property of Bantam Books and will not be returned under any circumstances.

2. Six men will be chosen by the Loveswept authors as a HOMETOWN HUNK (one HUNK per Loveswept title). By entering the contest, each winner and each person who enters a winner agrees to abide by Bantam Books' rules and to be subject to Bantam Books' eligibility requirements. Each winning HUNK and each person who enters a winner will be required to sign all papers deemed necessary by Bantam Books before receiving any prize. Each winning HUNK will be flown via **United Airlines** from his closest United Airlines-serviced city to New York City and will stay at the ꟼ St.SS.rr Hotel—the ideal hotel for business or pleasure in midtown Manhattan— for two nights. Winning HUNKS' meals and hotel transfers will be provided by Bantam Books. Travel and hotel arrangements are made by *RELIABLE TRAVEL INTERNATIONAL, INC.* and are subject to availability and to Bantam Books' date requirements. Each winning HUNK will pose with a female model at a photographer's studio for a photograph that will serve as the basis of a Loveswept front cover. Each winning HUNK will receive a $150.00 modeling fee. Each winning HUNK will be required to sign an Affidavit of Eligibility and Model's Release supplied by Bantam Books. (Approximate retail value of HOMETOWN HUNK'S PRIZE: $900.00). The six people who send in a winning HOMETOWN HUNK photograph that is used by Bantam will receive free for one year each, LOVESWEPT romance paperback books published by Bantam during that year. (Approximate retail value: $180.00.) Each person who submits a winning photograph

will also be required to sign an Affidavit of Eligibility and Promotional Release supplied by Bantam Books. All winning HUNKS' (as well as the people who submit the winning photographs) names, addresses, biographical data and likenesses may be used by Bantam Books for publicity and promotional purposes without any additional compensation. There will be no prize substitutions or cash equivalents made.

3. All completed entries must be received by Bantam Books no later than September 15, 1988. Bantam Books is not responsible for lost or misdirected entries. The finalists will be selected by Loveswept editors and the six winning HOMETOWN HUNKS will be selected by the six authors of the participating Loveswept books. Winners will be selected on the basis of how closely the judges believe they reflect the descriptions of the books' heroes. Winners will be notified on or about October 31, 1988. If there are insufficient entries or if in the judges' opinions, no entry is suitable or adequately reflects the descriptions of the hero(s) in the book(s), Bantam may decide not to award a prize for the applicable book(s) and may reissue the book(s) at its discretion.

4. The contest is open to residents of the U.S. and Canada, except the Province of Quebec, and is void where prohibited by law. All federal and local regulations apply. Employees of Reliable Travel International, Inc., United Airlines, the Summit Hotel, and the Bantam Doubleday Dell Publishing Group, Inc., their subsidiaries and affiliates, and their immediate families are ineligible to enter.

5. For an extra copy of the Official Rules, the Official Entry Form, and the accompanying Loveswept cover notes, send your request and a self-addressed stamped envelope (Vermont and Washington State residents need not affix postage) before August 20, 1988 to the address listed in Paragraph 1 above.

LOVESWEPT ᴸ HOMETOWN HUNK OFFICIAL ENTRY FORM

BANTAM BOOKS
HOMETOWN HUNK CONTEST
Dept. CN
666 Fifth Avenue
New York, New York 10102–0023

HOMETOWN HUNK CONTEST

YOUR NAME_____

YOUR ADDRESS_____

CITY_____ STATE_____ ZIP_____

THE NAME OF THE LOVESWEPT BOOK FOR WHICH YOU ARE ENTERING THIS PHOTO

_____by_____

YOUR RELATIONSHIP TO YOUR HERO_____

YOUR HERO'S NAME_____

YOUR HERO'S ADDRESS_____

CITY_____ STATE_____ ZIP_____

YOUR HERO'S TELEPHONE #_____

YOUR HERO'S DATE OF BIRTH_____

YOUR HERO'S SIGNATURE CONSENTING TO HIS PHOTOGRAPH ENTRY

_____